DRIVE ME CRAZY
REBEL PR BOOK 2

SUSAN HARRIS

Originally published as Kindle Vella Episodes

Cover Design by: Gem Promotions
Typography by: Gem Promotions

PROLOGUE

Jack

JACK SLAMMED his hand onto the dashboard as his Da swerved around another car, blaring the horn. Jack twisted in his seat to check on his Ma. Her face was contorted in pain, her hand on her stomach as blood soaked the towel he had given her to sit on so his Da wouldn't shout at her for messing up the backseat.

He was terrified. Absolutely terrified.

He was sure that his Ma was losing his baby sister and no matter how fast his Da drove to get to the hospital. Jack was certain that the pints and probably chasers his Da had drank down the pub wasn't helping his erratic driving. Especially in the goddamn rain.

"Da, slow down. You'll fucking kill us all."

"Don't tell me how to drive, ya smart shit." His Da snarled at him, his words slurred before he mounted a footpath, and cars blared their horns at him.

This was a disaster. His Da was drunk, his Ma was bleeding to death. His Da went through another red light and a Kia nearly went right into the side of them as his Ma cried out in pain. The car veered across lanes, and Jack wasn't sure how the guards hadn't shown up to arrest his Da.

"Da, pull over and let me fucking drive. You're gonna get us all killed."

His Ma let out a roar and was now bawling her eyes out.

"Shut up, Jack or I will throw ya out of this goddamn car while it's moving!"

His Da turned to him, taking one hand off the wheel like he was gonna smack him, but it only set the already veering car closer to the median of the dual carriageway. Jack reached out past his Da, grabbed the wheel, and gave it a yank.

Everything seemed to happen then in slow motion. His Da let go of the wheel but seemed to put his foot down on the accelerator. Jack tried to scramble to get a firm grip on the wheel, but his Da knocked his hands away.

The car headed straight toward the wall. His Ma was screaming. Jack had a moment to consider that he was about to die when the wall was suddenly there, and the car went into it at speed.

Jack heard a scream of metal and then his world went black.

CHAPTER ONE

Jack

NINE YEARS Later

Jack fucking hated weddings.

He could never understand why two people would tie themselves to one another and proclaim to love one another forever. They remained blissful for like ten years, then started to hate one another. Bad habits started to grate on nerves. Things that were cute in the honeymoon phase, absolutely wrecked your head until you were on the verge of getting your own Netflix crime documentary for murdering your significant other.

Jack had a right to be so cynical. Life liked to fuck him over time and time again. His parents had a volatile relationship. Everyone said that they had been teenage sweethearts so in love. But his Da liked a drink, and he was a mean drunk. He shouted and screamed until he passed out.

And that was a good night.

Jack's only means of escape had been karting. He'd saved any pocket money during the week and then went karting on a

Saturday morning. It was there Philip Coyle had seen him and offered him a chance at doing it for a living as a Formula 1 driver. His dad had been thrilled because Philip paid Jack a wage to drive karts for him, and his Da had more money to hand over to the barman.

There was a way out for Jack. He could almost grab hold of it. He would move out and live his dream and get out from the toxic environment that was his home life. Jack would try and persuade his Ma to leave his Da, but no matter how drunk he could get, she still loved the gobshite.

That dream had come to a fucking dead end the night his Da had gotten behind the wheel of his car, drunk off his ass and robbed everyone in the goddamn car of something solid in their future.

They had been driving to the hospital because his mam had gone into labour. She was early, too damn early and his Da had spent the day getting drunk after watching the six nations. Jack had only been fifteen but had tried to get his Da to give him the keys so he could drive them, but Tommy O'Neill said he was grand and to shut the hell up. That his Ma was whinging enough for the both of them.

The rain had been hammering down outside as they drove to the hospital. Jack was in the passenger seat, his Ma in the back as his Da drove like a maniac in the torrential rain. He'd yelled at his Da to slow down. His Da had laughed and kicked the speed up a gear. Then his Da started to veer over to the lane with the oncoming traffic and Jack had grabbed the wheel.

After that, things got a little blurry.

When Jack woke up, the social worker told him that his Ma said that him and his Da had fought over the wheel, and when his Da had gotten control, the car had slammed straight into a wall. The wall had collapsed on top of the car, crushing it and they all had to be cut out of the car unconscious.

Or in his Da's case.... dead.

Because Tommy O'Neill was too much of a man to wear a seatbelt.

A fucking dumbass is what he was.

Because his Da had neglected to wear a seatbelt, his body had been flung round and caused irreparable internal damage. The crushed skull hadn't helped either. And his Ma, she had lost the baby girl she'd so desperately wanted. The doctors couldn't confirm if the baby died because of the crash or if the crash was a factor. His Ma had blamed him for months after they got out of hospital, because maybe if Jack hadn't tried to wrestle control of the wheel, his Da and his baby sister would still be alive.

Jack's world had been turned upside down after the crash and the freedom he'd craved with a career that would take him all over the world was sawed off along with his right leg.

Jack blinked his eyes a couple of times to try and rid himself of the fog. His head hurt. Hell, his entire body hurt. He let out a moan, his voice sounding weird. He felt like he was dying with a hangover like the time he'd drank that Polish vodka his classmate had brought to a party.

"Jack, can you hear me?"

Christ, why did people have to talk so damn loud.

Jack focused on the man's voice, listened as he introduced himself as a social worker, and then explained to Jack that he had been in a car crash. Apparently, Jack had been unconscious for the past month recovering. Jack's brain was fuzzy, and he was only taking in a little of what the social worker was telling him.

Where was his Ma? His Da was probably propped up at a bar somewhere, not giving a shit about Jack. When Jack asked after his Ma, the social worker glanced at the floor and his heart started to race.

"Where's me Ma?" Jack demanded, his voice sounding sluggish.

"Your mother is resting at home with your aunt. We called her and told her you are awake."

Jack wanted to ask after the baby, and it was on the tip of his tongue to ask but the social worker looked away and shifted in his seat. Jack knew then that his baby sister hadn't survived the crash and his chest ached.

What a fucking mess...what a right fucking mess.

"Jack, we do need to talk to you about something." He lifted his hand and a doctor came in. Jack saw the expression on the doctor's face, knew something terrible was coming, but there was no preparing for the blow that was about to hit him smack bang in the chest.

"Jack," The doctor started after introducing himself. "We wanted your mother to be here to tell you about what happened after the car crash, but as you've woken up, we can't delay this any longer."

He tried to sit up in the bed, felt a little off balance and then his eyes landed on his legs...

"Your leg was crushed in the collision, Jack. You were bleeding out and they were left with no option but to remove the limb to free you from the vehicle."

Jack couldn't stop looking at his legs.

"You put it back on, right? Like they do on the telly?" He hated the pleading in his tone.

The doctor gave a shake of her head. "I'm very sorry, Jack. There was no saving your leg."

Jack ripped the blankets off his body and looked down to where his right leg came to a halt just above the knee. He stared at it, the space where his leg used to be and then suddenly, someone was screaming and screaming.

It took Jack a few minutes to realize that the person screaming was him.

He'd lost his shit then, trashing the place and cursing his Da, and because his Ma blamed him for everything, it had been up to the social worker and the doctor to tell him that his Da had died in the crash. Jack had been glad, in the heat of the moment. Glad the fucker was dead because he had ruined his life.

Jack scrubbed a hand down his face and took a large gulp of his beer. He looked around, uncomfortable, and not really sure why he was standing here in a suit. Well, he knew why. His boss, F1 World Champion, Noah Donovan had invited him to the impromptu wedding. Having proposed a while ago, and with a baby on the way, Noah and Charlie Coyle, had decided that they wanted to get married before Noah went off to defend his title.

They had gathered everyone to their back garden, and the couple had said their vows right there instead of opting for a massive event. The bash was still star-studded, with rockstar best men and PR mogul maids of honour.

Jack wasn't sure why Noah had invited him, or why Luke Sullivan, his rally teammate had told him that he had to go because Noah was trying to make him feel like part of the family.

Everyone was having great craic. But since Jack hardly knew anyone, he was standing anyone; lemon by himself to the side. The only one who looked more miserable than Jack felt was Hollywood Heartthrob, Joshua James.

Jack had watched him the entire night, and when he thought no one was watching him, and the man looked lost. And as someone who had felt lost for a long time, Jack knew sadness when he saw it. JJ looked at him, blinked, then lifted his whiskey glass in greeting before he turned back to rockstar Oli Scott, and Jack could see how good an actor the other man was.

He too, knew a thing or two about pretending.

CHAPTER TWO

Jack

JACK STRETCHED in bed and opened his eyes to stare at the ceiling. He'd managed to get a few hours sleep in between the nightmare and the restlessness that was weighing him down. Too much thinking about the past always made him feel off balance which was funny considering he was literally always off balance.

He'd made a very Irish exit from the party last night, shooting Luke a text to say he was bailing, but his teammate hadn't even glanced in his direction as he danced with his boyfriend, Danish soccer star, Emil Anderson. They looked so sickly in love that Jack's teeth ached.

Reaching over, he grabbed his phone to see two missed calls from his Ma, and about a half dozen messages. Jack exhaled and put the phone back on the bedside table. He loved his Ma, he really did, but her way of overcompensating for blaming him for the accident rather than blame the asshole who had gotten behind the wheel drunk was to suffocate him.

"If you hadn't of grabbed the wheel my husband and baby would be alive!"

That was exactly what she had roared at him at the foot of his hospital bed as he tried to come to terms with the fact that he was missing a limb. It had taken her three days after he had woken up for her to come see him, and when she had and all Jack wanted was for his Ma to hug him and tell him he'd be okay, he'd taken one look at her face and had known she blamed him for the accident.

It was Philip Coyle who had come to the hospital and hugged Jack when he had broken down. It was Philip who had paid for a private rehab for Jack to come to terms with his new life, and Philip who came to visit him.

But when he had returned home, his Ma had started to try and make amends for what she had said by trying to do everything for him. Jack had learned to be self-sufficient in the time he'd been away. He didn't need his Ma's help to look after himself. He'd carried on his schooling and had completed his Leaving Cert by the time he'd come home.

Philip had arranged for him to do a mechanics apprenticeship and it was brilliant and painful at the same time because all Jack wanted to do was drive. His boss must have seen the look in Jack's eyes when he serviced the supped-up rally cars, because one day he had come out and shown Jack a video of drivers who had disabilities but still had successful driving careers.

For the first time since the accident, Jack had felt hopeful that he could still have a career in racing. Maybe not Formula 1 like he had dreamed of, but he didn't really care once he was driving. His Ma had been livid and had immediately forbidden him from doing it.

Jack worked his ass of to get his fitness back on track. He worked out and made sure his upper body was strong and his remaining leg too. He qualified as a mechanic, bought a

Subaru Impreza WRX, and kitted it out with the help of the other mechanics at the garage he worked in.

The hardest part was trying to convince rally teams that he was capable of driving. He entered a few amateur competitions, and won a few with his modified car, but he couldn't get an offer. The excuses flew in. Insurance would be too high. It was too dangerous. He'd never get sponsorship.

Blah, blah, fucking blah.

That had only made Jack more determined and when Rebel Racers had held an open track day, Jack had entered and driven his car like he'd stolen it. He ignored the stares and the pitiful glances as he took off his everyday prosthesis and attached his special, fucking expensive driving leg. That all faded away the moment the lights went out and he pressed down on the accelerator.

He clocked the fastest time out of all the rally drivers, and got a shiny medal in all for it, but Jack had only been interested in getting noticed by the teams who were there as spectators. When no one approached him at the end of the day, Jack was fuming and was about to throw in the towel when he'd been approached by Noah Donovan.

Jack slammed the boot of the car down and swore, his anger like fucking fire in his veins. He was fit to murder the able-bodied pricks for being so fucking clueless that he was the best driver they could ever hope to hire.

"Nice car."

Jack glanced up to see F1 superstar Noah Donovan standing there looking at him. He was wearing his team hoodie and Jack had a fanboy moment before he reigned in the urge to ask the damn racer for a bloody selfie.

Jack patted the car. "Keiko's better than just nice. She's a beast."

Noah grinned, then looked over his shoulder. "I think the corporate assholes are missing a trick with you."

Jack gave a little shrug of his shoulders. "Doesn't matter. No matter how fucking brilliantly I drive, the moment they remember that I come with missing parts, they don't give a fuck." He looked over to where Noah's Formula 1 car was on display. "I wanted to be you. Philip had me convinced I could be the next you. I really don't know who I am if I'm not a driver."

He wasn't used to talking to complete strangers about his feelings, and yet, he knew that Noah would understand. Racing was in his blood, just like it was in Jack's, and that would never change.

Noah folded his arms across his chest. "Come race for me."

Jack's eyebrows shot up. What the fuck?

With a chuckle, Noah shifted his weight from one foot to the other. "Listen, I can see how talented you are. I saw the videos Philip had of you and you're faster now than you were when you had two legs."

Noah wasn't being cruel to Jack. He was just stating facts so Jack would understand his bluntness.

"I'm investing in a rally team. It's new and there is a lot of paperwork that I can tell you frustrates the hell out of me, but I want you as one of my drivers. And before you ask, it's not a pity hire or anything. I want the best drivers and you have what it takes to be a rally champion."

Jack wasn't sure what was happening, but when he woke up this morning, he hadn't expected this. He had no qualms in reaching down to pinch his other arm.

"I promise this is real," Noah replied, glancing over his shoulder to where Jack saw a beautiful black-haired woman walking around Noah's car and the other man grinned. "And I'm not gonna lie and tell you that you'll be competing next week if you want in. It might take a while. But the shot is there if you wanna take it."

Jack had wanted to throw his arms around Noah and thank him, but he'd nodded, asking Noah if he could think about it. Noah had nodded his approval, exchanging details and Noah promised to send over a contract so Jack could look it over. Then Noah had explained to him that he was hoping that the second driver would be Luke Sullivan, his former teammate who had nearly died in a crash and had some issues with his hip that prevented him from being in F1.

That intrigued Jack.

He'd met with Noah twice more to hash things out before signing the contract. They'd made the official announcement through Rebel PR, the company Noah's now wife and her best friend ran. They'd recently added Shane Carter as a partner, and he was head of the sports department, and Jack had to admit that Shane knew what he was talking about.

His Ma had been livid. She had phoned him up and ranted for a solid half hour about the dangers of rally driving, shutting up when Jack just said that he'd already lost one limb, but he had a few going spare. The phone had disconnected then, and he'd had a blissful week of no contact.

He moved to sit at the edge of the bed, reaching for his knee sleeve and rolled it onto this stump. It ached a little, but Jack would have a look at it later. He wanted to get to the gym and work out before his slot on the sim at Rebel Racers. Because NLQ Racing had no base of operations yet, they were using the Rebel Racers facilities.

Once his prosthetic was secured, Jack pushed off the bed and stood, giving himself a minute to adjust. That was how his life was in a nutshell. Jack spent a lot of time giving himself a minute to adjust, and sometimes, you just had to put one foot in front of the other...even if one of those feet wasn't real.

Chapter Three

Karla

As the plane began its descent into Dublin, Karla starred out the window. It was rather green, just like they had described on social media as she tried to prepare herself for this massive change in her life. Moving from Denmark to Ireland hadn't been a whim or a rash choice for Karla. She had weighed up the pros and cons, and when Shane Carter of Rebel PR had made her an offer she couldn't refuse, Karla had packed up her life and booked a one-way ticket.

Of course, she had worried that the job was offered to her simply because of her of who her brother was. Shane had assured her that he'd been impressed with her CV and that his decision to hire Karla had nothing to do with her brother. Karla hadn't been sure if she believed him, but the opportunity had been too good to turn down.

Karla was used to being known as Emil Anderson's little sister. Her brother was a legend in Denmark, having played for their national football team since he was a teenager and had captained for almost two years now. Recently, about the time he was made captain, Emil had made Karla so proud when he came out as bisexual and the world had embraced him.

Her brother was now in a committed relationship with Luke Sullivan, a former Formula 1 star turned rally driver. They lived together in Ireland but spent time in Denmark and the UK where Emil played his club football.

Emil had been the rock of their family after their father's accident, and no one would have expected a boy from a small fishing village would be world-famous. Karla remembered how Emil used to go out in the snow wearing his hiking boots and practice kicking a ball against the wall of snow. He did that with any spare time he had, up at the crack of dawn to work before school.

Her brother had wanted his sisters to have the best opportunities, so he had paid for both Karla and their sister Lærke to go to college. Karla had chosen public relations and sports management, while Lærke had gone for an arts degree. Lærke was younger than Karla by a year, but her sister had married young to her childhood sweetheart and was now expecting her first child.

Emil had helped Karla get a job with the Danish National team when Oskar, Emil's best friend had left to take a role within Rebel Racers. It had been amazing working with the youth team, but Karla had felt the pressure to be like Lærke and settle down by her mother.

Karla would never, ever tell Emil what had happened in the argument that had ensued when Karla had told their mother that she was moving to Ireland for a job, where her mother had been shocked and angry about Karla leaving. Her mother wanted Karla to stay in Denmark, marry a nice Danish man, and give her grandchildren, especially since her only son would probably never now give her a grandchild.

It had shocked both her and Lærke, considering their mother had been so supportive of Emil coming out and had welcomed Luke with open arms. Karla had then told her mother that she wanted to experience the world before she settled down and made a joke that she was following in their ancestor's footsteps by travelling to Ireland.

Needless to say, Karla had taken herself to the airport this morning to embark on her new adventure. Of course, she was nervous. Fuck that, she was terrified. She had left a good job and the only home she had always known to start over. She would be living on her own for the first time in her life and it was both daunting and exciting at the same time.

The plane landed and Karla disembarked, then went to collect her cases. Karla strode out of the arrivals door and glanced around. She spotted a familiar tinge of red hair, though, since she was in Ireland it might not have been the redhead she was looking for.

The crowds parted and then, her brother was striding toward her, a big grin on his face as he held the hand of his red-haired boyfriend. Emil had dark hair and eyes, was similar in height to her, and was slim and muscular. It was no wonder men and woman looked in his direction, even if you set aside the fact that he was a famous footballer.

Emil let go of his boyfriend's hand to come and embrace her, lifting her off her feet as she laughed, the unease she had felt easing now that she was in her brother's arms. When Emil set her down, he brushed the hair from her face and said in Danish. "I have missed you little sister."

Karla smiled wider. "You only saw me two weeks ago. And you are the one heading off in a few days again."

Emil switched to English. "But now Luke can keep an eye on you for me and make sure you are staying out of trouble. He's used to having to watch Luna."

The other man laughed, then came forward to give Karla a hug. Then Luke took one of her cases and after pausing so Emil and Luke could sign a few autographs and take a few photos, they were in Luke's car and driving down the motorway to Cork.

"Thank you for coming to get me, Luke."

Luke smiled at her in the mirror. "No hassle. I've been training so hard in my new rally car that it was nice to go for a spin in a normal car. Might have gotten a speeding ticket though on the way up but it'll be grand."

Karla laughed as she watched Emil reach out and rest his hand on Luke's thigh. It was such a comfortable gesture, and even though Karla knew their road to being this open was hard, she was glad that Emil had Luke and Luke had Emil. When Emil had opened up about his sexuality, Karla had felt saddened that Emil hadn't felt like he could tell her about that part of him.

It had been Oskar, her brother's best friend and Karla's childhood crush who had told her that Emil had not told him either, and that was not what they should dwell on. What mattered was that Emil had found a man that he loved enough to be open about his sexuality, and that Emil was happy.

"You know you could have stayed with us," Emil said from the front of the car.

Karla turned to look out the window, and watched the outside world, the scenery so different to what she was so used to. "I know. But the apartment comes with the job. And I will be only a few steps away from where I work. I will never know if I can be independent if I do not try."

As she dragged her gaze from looking out the window, Karla saw that Emil was looking at her. Her brother frowned, then sighed. "I spoke to Lærke. She told me mother wasn't speaking to you."

"Lærke should not have told you. We hate it when you and mom quarrel."

The fact of it was that Emil had been more than a brother to her, he had almost been more a father, since theirs had not been the same since his accident and Emil had to work to provide for the family. It was not Emil's responsibility to parent her and she had to learn to stand on her own to feet without having him to lean on.

It was enough to know that he would be there if she happened to fall.

"Mother will come around. It is hard for her to see us so far away. And Lærke has always been fiercely independent. Mother expected to keep you close for a long time."

Karla snorted. "She was trying to marry me off. I think the fact Lærke defied the odds and married the boy next door made her want to marry me off to anyone who would have me. She told me I was too outspoken to be a good wife."

Luke barked out a laugh. "Speaking as someone who has a sister who is the most outspoken person I know, you are tame. Last week at family dinner, Luna told our parents that she had been trying to persuade Cathal to get a Prince Albert from the new piercer at the shop because she had heard that the orgasms were some epic shit and planned on asking Oli's fiancé all about it."

Karla's mouth went wide in shock. "What did your parents say?"

"Well, Cathal went the same colour as the ketchup, my mam told Luna that was too much information, and my dad just shrugged."

"Maybe we should send Luna to have a word with mother?" Emil suggested, his eyes dancing with mischief.

Everyone laughed and Karla finally started to believe that maybe she could grow to call Ireland home.

CHAPTER FOUR

Karla

KARLA HAD an amazing weekend spent with Emil and Luke. She stayed with them until she went to work on Monday and got the keys to her new apartment. They had taken her around Cork, then to the beach, showing her some of the sights. Then Luke had introduced her to chips and curry sauce, and when he had buttered his bread and then put the chips and curry into his bread, Karla had been appalled until she tried it herself.

Now it was her new favourite thing.

Karla had fallen asleep early on Saturday, retiring to Emil and Luke's spare room to give the couple time together since Emil was leaving on Monday. She had been dead to the world by the time her head hit the pillow. When she had gotten up the next morning, Luke had claimed that it was the sea air that had done her in.

After Karla had showered and dressed, they had all gone to Luke's family home, which was beside the family business, a delightful pub on the outskirts of the city. Luke's parents had made her feel so welcome, hugging her as if she wasn't a stranger, but like one of the family.

Luke's twin sister, Luna, had stood off to the side and Karla had the distinct impression that the woman with the bloodred hair was sizing her up. Karla had never felt so under the microscope. It wasn't until Luna's partner, a tattoo artist with a name it took Karla a few attempts to say properly, nudged Luna and told her to behave.

The slow smile had transformed Luna's face, as she walked over and slung an arm across Karla's shoulders. "I always wanted a sister. I used to dress Luke up and pretend he was my sister Lisa."

"Jesus, Luna, shut up."

They all had laughed, sitting down for dinner. Karla had smiled and spoken at times, but for the most part, she had taken in what it must have been like to have dinner like this every Sunday. She loved her mother, but her father hadn't been himself for years after his accident. Emil had already gone away to play football, and Lærke had made sure that she spent as little time at home as possible, leaving Karla to be the one to make sure her parents ate, and then when her father had died, making sure her mother was looked after.

Karla had allowed Lærke to find herself for years...now it was Karla's time to try and figure out who she was.

After the dinner, they had all gone into the pub, Luke's dad Mick asking Karla what she liked to drink, but Karla had never been much of a drinker. He regarded her for a moment, then poured her a glass of cider, and when Karla took a sip so as not to be rude, found that the sharp taste was quite refreshing.

When it was time to leave, Karla watched as Emil was embraced by Luke's parents, and that made her smile, because after all Emil had done for his family, it was nice to see his boyfriend's family care about him so much. Karla had been shocked when they had shown her the exact same care, with Luke and Luna's mum telling her that even when Emil and Luke were away working, she always had family only a phone call or a visit away.

If only her own mother had been so warm.

"You look just how you used to whenever you had too many thoughts in your head."

Karla turned to look at her brother's profile as he drove her to Rebel PR. He had offered to drop her off this morning before he headed to the airport. She had felt so guilty that Luke and Emil's last weekend together for a while had been consumed with her arrival. Emil had reassured her that they didn't mind, and that Luke would be over to see him in a couple of weeks, and maybe she could come too since it had been ages since Karla had seen him play.

Emil pulled into a car park space, turned off the engine and looked at Karla. "Are you sure this is what you want, lillesøster?"

Karla smiled at Emil, the familiar term of endearment reminding her of when she was a child and idolized her big brother. "I'm okay. I promise. It's just a lot to process but this is what I want. I know you are probably sad that I left the Danish team but that was an easy role. I wanted a challenge. I craved adventure."

Emil regarded Karla and ran a hand through his dark hair. "It is my fault that you had your wings clipped. I never felt like I had to worry about you because you were the sensible one, the one who had her feet firmly planted on solid ground. I should never have left you to parent our parents."

Karla has already started shaking her head while Emil was speaking. "No. You had to go because you, dearest Emil, were not made to spend your life on a fishing boat. I made the selfish decision because I was afraid of becoming our mother. I did not want to spend my life in a tiny village, married to a fisherman, and become bitter when my children leave me to see the world I never did."

Karla blinked at how harsh she sounded, and it had Emil narrowing his gaze and looking at her in a way he did when he was trying to figure out something that she or Lærke had done something mischievous and had gotten in trouble.

She reached over and rested a hand on his arm. "I promise you that I am fine. Luke is going to bring over my cases later once I have the keys and meet my first client. And you heard Luna's mum yesterday. We have a coffee date to go shopping for things to make me feel at home."

Emil didn't look convinced, so Karla gave him a hug, kissed his cheek, then opened the car door. "I will see you soon, brother. Safe travels. Love you."

"I love you too, Karla. Call me if you need me."

Karla got out of the car and headed into the building that had the Rebel PR logo on the outside. She took a moment to look at all the famous clientele, including her brother. She stopped and blinked at the picture of Shane Carter, who Karla had not known had been an Olympian.

"No matter how many times I ask Andi to take that down, she refuses."

Karla turned to see Shane leaning against the reception counter, a smile on his face. she glanced at the photo and back to him. "I think you made a mistake hiring me. I might have worked with the Danish team, but I am not sporty."

"Hey neither is Andi, but she does alright. Besides, you know more about that side of it than she does. We wouldn't have agreed to hire ya if you didn't have the right qualifications and experience. Your references speak for themselves, and I need someone who can handle a difficult client with ease."

Karla snorted, knowing full well that working for a men's football team as a woman had several challenges, though they were ones that Karla had been able to handle with ease. She followed Shane into the main area, where he showed Karla her desk, and gave her the keys to her new apartment. When the metal landed in the palm of her hand, Karla felt a little thrill of excitement course through her.

"Your apartment is across the way from mine. Eve, my girl-friend, used to stay there until we moved in together. Andi said feel free to do whatever you want to the place, and if you buy any furniture or anything, Rebel PR will reimburse you."

"Oh, you don't have to do that." Karla argued, but Shane shook his head.

"All part of the perks of working for Rebel PR."

Karla had a feeling that she was going to like it at Rebel PR.

"You didn't say who my first client was gonna be." Karla said as she looked around the office. Shane smiled a kind of secretive smile that had Karla wondering what Shane had up his sleeves.

"I think you need to meet him first. See if you want to take him on."

Karla rested her hands on her hips and tilted her head to the side. "When can I meet him?"

Shane checked the smartwatch on his wrist. "He's supposed to be at Rebel Racers for the rest of the day. We can head there now if you're sure you want to get stuck in straight away. But meeting him can wait a few days if you wanna get settled."

"I'm ready to get stuck in. I can settle in later tonight when Luke brings over my stuff."

Shane nodded his approval, made a quick phone call to tell Andi that they were heading out and they'd come back after so Andi could meet Karla. Then they headed out to wherever the client was and Karla felt a spike of anxiety, pushing it down and reminding herself that she could do this.

Chapter Five

Jack

Jack never felt more at home than when he was in a car...or under one for that matter. This morning he'd enjoyed his workout, and after showering in the Rebel Racers facilities, spent up until lunchtime working in the simulator. Charlie had stopped by, telling him it felt weird to be here when the place felt so empty.

While there was a lot of staff still onsite who worked remotely with the team who travelled, a lot of Charlie's close staff were on the road with Noah and Quinn. Jack knew it must be hard to be separated from your new husband while being very pregnant. When his time on the sim was up, Jack had asked Charlie if there was any chance he could work on his car while it was being held in the garage.

Charlie had been delighted, telling him she was gonna be in her office all afternoon doing paperwork and stuff, and she'd get someone to get him an access pass so Jack could come and go as he pleased. Jack wasn't sure what to say to that and it must have showed on his face because Charlie just laughed and patted his shoulder.

"It's for purely selfish reasons, really. If you are working on the car then I can listen to the roar of the engine, smell oil and diesel and all the good stuff when I'm stuck here and not on a racetrack."

Jack was used to people being fake nice to him because of his leg. The lads in school, girls who thought him handsome and were curious about his leg. After the crash, most of his friends had bailed, because Jack was no longer going to be a famous F1 racer. He had spent a lot of time by himself, even though he wasn't a hermit or anything, he'd dated, but the allure of dating him wore off after a time so he'd just stopped.

So when Charlie made him the offer, Jack had fully expected there to be like some ulterior motive. However, Charlie seemed genuinely happy to have him around, and when Noah called her, she told him that she'd been hanging with Jack and she wasn't here all alone.

Being in the garage of a Formula 1 world champion should be daunting as fuck, but Noah's side of the garage was kitted out with everything he needed to work on his car. He'd driven the rally car onto the lift, raised it a little, and then gotten down on the mechanic's creeper to go under the car.

Noah had told Jack that they had mechanics who would help out on the cars, but Jack told him that he could do the heavy lifting himself, since he was a qualified mechanic. His new boss had been a little hesitant, reluctant even, until Jack had pointed to Luke's car as his teammate tested out his new seat adjustments and told Noah the brakes needed checking.

And sure enough, the brake pads were worn down and needed replacing.

Noah had conceded, though he did tell Jack that he would need mechanics on hand so that he could concentrate on driving when they finally started racing. Also, before he left,

Noah had given him and Luke a list of possible navigators, and he was to have a conversation with Luke to discuss the options in the next few weeks.

Jack slid out and grabbed the tools he needed, but stopped as his phone rang. Pulling it from his pocket, he sighed when he saw his Ma's name light up, silenced the call, then connected his phone to the speaker and cranked the music, before sliding back under the car.

"You can't be serious, Jack."

Jack didn't need his Ma nagging him about his decision. He wasn't a child and Philip Coyle had been good to him since well before the accident. He didn't want to be constantly reminded of all the things he couldn't do. Jack didn't need to be told that he wasn't the same boy he once was and his life was no longer exactly what he'd expected to be.

But his Ma hadn't got the memo. Daily she reminded him of the night that had changed their lives forever. And then when she wasn't reminding him about his lost limb, his Ma was smothering him with affection.

Jack knew it wasn't genuine. It was because of what she had said to him when she had finally rocked up to the hospital, blaming him and not her drunk of a husband. After he'd thought about it, Jack had felt sorry for her. She'd lost her baby, her husband, and ended up with a disabled son.

And yet, Jack knew, every time his Ma looked at him, no matter how many presents or gifts, or proclamations of love that she offered to him, Jack could see it in her eyes that he was a burden to her. And she still blamed him for the accident.

"I'm deadly serious, Ma. Philip got me the apprenticeship. The gaff comes with the job. The lads at the garage are gonna kit it out and make it more accessible for me. I can get out of this house, earn a wage, and be around people who don't look at me like a goddamn, fucking cripple."

"Jack, lad, no one thinks that."

Jack shoved some clothes into his duffel. *"Ma, you look at me like that. All the kids in school did. The teachers too. But when I'm at the garage, no one gives a fuck that my right leg is detachable. No one feels sorry for me if I can't pull my weight, and they tease me like they do everyone else."*

His Ma shook her head. *"You should have applied to some colleges like I wanted you to. You could have had a nice career, made some money. If you'd focused on your studies instead of tinkering with cars, you might have gotten into a good course."*

Ah, that old chestnut...his Ma making out that he was smart enough to get into a poxy law course or what, become a doctor? Could ya imagine it, him, a doctor...sure no one would ever want him to do surgery once they got a sconce at his missing leg...

Not exactly great advertising for doctors, was it?

"Enough, Ma." Jack said as he zipped up his duffel and slung it over his shoulder. *"I've made me decision and that's it. You can argue with me all ya want but I'm moving out and you can't stop me."*

"You're making a mistake."

But Jack had proved her wrong, hadn't he?

Aslan's *Crazy World* came on and Jack smiled, belting out the lyrics like he was main staging a concert. Not that he could sing like. He was sure that if there was a God, he or she had decided to not give him any semblance of a good voice because Jack had already been blessed with killer driving skills, and a handsome face.

Jack was singing his heart out, and bopping away to the music when he heard a double knock on the bonnet of the car. Sliding out, Jack spotted Shane Carter, Rebel PR's sports guru, and one of the hottest women Jack had ever seen in his life.

Dark brunette hair that was long and curly, hung loose around her shoulders. She was slim, but clad in jeans, making

Jack want her to turn around so he could see if her ass was as curvy as he thought it would be. Her eyes were dark just like her hair, making her flawless skin look creamier. Her lips were full, like she was pouting, and Jack wondered if they would feel as soft as they looked if he kissed her.

What the hell was he thinking?

Despite the fact that the woman was drop dead gorgeous, her outfit told Jack that she was trying to be all professional. Skintight jeans and a pair of court shoes, the woman wore a blouse tucked into her jeans, and a blazer over it. She was staring down at him, chewing on her bottom lip like she was nervous.

Jack hoped that Shane wasn't trying to pawn off this woman on him as his new babysitter. They had talked about it, and Jack had protested, then agreed to consider it in the long run. Guess the long run was today.

He wouldn't be opposed to flirting with her if she wasn't here to order him about and nag him and shit...he already got that from his Ma. But he *could* try and annoy the fuck out of her or scare her off, couldn't he?

Withdrawing his phone to turn off the music, Jack let a long, slow, smile curve his lips as he arched his brow, and gave the woman one long assessing appraisal before pushing up on his elbows as he turned to Shane, the other man watching Jack with a cautious expression.

"Carter, man, my birthday's not for another couple of months. Ya didn't need to bring me a stripper. But I can't say I don't appreciate it.

Chapter Six

Karla

For a moment, Karla was afraid that this was something cultural that she was missing. Was stripper a term that was different here than in Denmark? She had been studying up on Irish culture since Emil had moved here to be with Luke, but there was still a lot of things that Karla had yet to understand. Was this one of those things that were just beyond her yet?

"Behave, Jack," Shane said, a warning in his tone.

The man grinned up at her, mischief gleaming in his green eyes. "Where's the fun in that, Shaney lad."

Anger and embarrassment flushed through her. So he had been calling her a stripper. How dare he? Karla was not unused to men and the way in which they spoke to and about women. It came part and parcel with working in sports. Danish men were more direct with their words, and did not need pretence and insults to speak to women.

Shane sighed, shaking his head as the man got to his feet and Karla got her first proper look at this racer who was to be her client. Black hair that was cut short at the sides but looked thicker on the top. Busy black brows over intense green eyes, and his lips were curved into a grin. He was lean, like a swimmer, much like Emil's Luke was.

He was infuriately handsome, and something told Karla that he knew it.

Jack grabbed a cloth from the side and gave his hands a clean. He had a black stain on his cheek, but it didn't seem to bother him at all. He studied her for a moment and Karla struggled not to squirm under the weight of his eyes.

His lips quirked, and then he looked at Shane. "So, what's up? No Eve this week so you gotta come look at my handsome face?"

"Eve's in Liverpool doing an intensive week of training. I was ordered to stay at home and not distract her. I'm sure she will be happy to kick your ass in the ring the moment she's back in town.

Jack slid his gaze to Karla, and she instantly tensed. "Does the MMA star know you're hanging out with her boyfriend? I'm sure she'd have something to say about that. While the cat's away and all that. Bold boy, Shaney."

What the hell? Was this man really suggesting that she was fooling around with Shane behind his girlfriend's back?

"Jack," Shane said in a chastising tone. "Watch your mouth."

But it did not restrain the man at all. Jack sort of sneered at Karla, mocking her as he said. "Don't you speak? Or do you not understand English? Should I talk a little slower for ya?"

Karla's hands clenched into fists as she glared at him. "Du er et røvhul."

Jack grinned. "I might be an asshole, sweetheart, but I'm an asshole who knows Danish swear words."

Karla's mouth hung open. She had not been expecting that. By the Gods, Shane must think she was very unprofessional calling her client an asshole when they hadn't even been introduced. This was an absolute disaster.

As if he saw it on her face, Shane gave her a reassuring smile. "He's always like this. You'll get used to him. Hell, the first conversation that he had with Eve she threatened to smack him upside the head. She called him far worse than an asshole. He does this to get a rise out of you."

"I'm standing right here, Shane lad."

Shane rolled his eyes. "You can see why I need your help."

Jack's eyes narrowed. "Help with what?"

"With you, ya numpty." Shane told him and Jack scowled, making Karla laugh.

Jack glared at her, and she shrugged her shoulders before saying. "I may not understand a lot of Irish mannerisms, but Luke has called Emil a numpty on a number of occasions, so I understand that one."

That had Shane laughing out loud, even as Jack frowned at Shane.

"She has you on that, mate. You should have been nicer."

Jack snorted, rolled his eyes, and then focused on Karla. "You know Luke and Emil."

Shane cleared his throat, then it was him who made the introductions. "Jack, let me introduce you to Karla Anderson. Karla, this is Jack O'Neill. As much of a smartass as he is, he is an excellent rally driver."

"Thanks, I guess," Jack grumbled, shifting on his feet, then he looked at Karla, his gaze narrowed. "Anderson? As in Emil Anderson? Are you related or something?"

Karla glanced at Shane, who gave her an encouraging smile. This was nothing new to Karla, having to explain who Karla was and who her brother was. But this Jack had already shown that he was quick to judgement, based on his stripper comment.

"Emil is my brother," Karla told him, and his eyes widened.

"Ahh, so Shane here is babysitting you while big brother is off kicking a ball about. I knew your accent sounded familiar."

"Not quite, Jack." Shane started, then folded his arms across his chest. "Karla here is Rebel PR's newest acquisition. She comes highly recommended by the Danish under 20's team, who were devasted to lose her."

"She could go back," Jack muttered and Karla sighed, drawing Jack's attention. "I'm sure if they loved her so much, they wouldn't mind taking her back after her nice holiday to Ireland."

"Since you have a real hard time controlling that smart mouth of yours, Karla will be handling all media and interview requests. She'll be part PA, part publicist, part promotions advisor. She will be sifting through the sponsorship offers that are coming in. And also helping to interview navigators for you and Luke."

Jack's face fell, and he moved away from the front of the car to one of the benches. "I'll tell you what I told Andi, what I said to that reporter wasn't me running my mouth. They asked me personal questions about me, then asked me about Luke. I told them to fuck off because I can't stand people who nose into others private business."

"You called him a homophobic prick and an unscrupulous bastard."

Karla did not want to find any reasons to like this Jack but knowing that he had stood up for her brother and his partner, made him calling her a stripper seem like something Karla could let go of.

"Was I wrong?" Jack asked Shane, leaning a hip against the bench. "Like who asks anyone if I felt uncomfortable showering with Luke. If Luke and Emil sharing a room made me feel uneasy. Did I think Luke was checking me out all the time? That's not being a journalist, that's being a dickhead."

"Tell Karla what you told the journalist then." Shane urged Jack.

"I told the røvhul that of course Luke was checking me out because I'm fucking gorgeous and how could he not. And I said that even though I didn't swing that way, if I was gonna go gay, then I'd happily join both Luke and Emil for a filthy threesome."

Karla barked out a laugh, shaking her head. "Did you tell Luke and Emil what you said?"

"Yup," Jack said as he grabbed a packet of crisps and opened them. "The moment I walked out of the interview since Luke was due to go in next and I didn't want him to face up to that. Luke went that hilarious shade of red he goes when anyone says anything remotely dirty, but Emil just laughed and told me that he was a one man kinda guy."

"And then Jack went on his video streaming channel and called out the journalist for being a homophobic prick causing uproar."

Jack gave a very unbothered shrug of his shoulders. "If you want an apology, then I'm not going to offer one. I'm not one for mincing my words, and I'm certainly not one for pandering to idiots who have outdated views on the world."

Karla regarded Jack with new eyes. For all his faults, and Karla was starting to believe that he had many, he did seem like a decent man. Emil had received an overwhelming show of support when he came out as bisexual and he and Luke as a couple had been welcomed with open arms by most.

However, there were still bigots, who did not like that Emil and Luke were being labelled as the new IT couple and put hateful things online. Karla had seen some of it, as had Emil and Luke. It made her feel appreciative that Luke had such an understanding teammate.

And one who would stand up for the shyer, coyer Luke.

"And I'm not gonna mince my words now." Jack continued, taking the time to eat some of his crisps, swallowing before he continued. "I don't need or want anyone to filter out requests for me. I don't need a minder. I don't need any PR consultant because I'm just gonna drive the car and that's it. So you can find Karla here some other person to babysit 'cause she sure as shit isn't gonna babysit me."

CHAPTER SEVEN

Jack

"Listen, Jack," Shane began, frowning as he continued, "It's a done deal. This has come from your bosses, so if you don't like it, you can try and take it up with Noah, Luke, and Quinn. But I don't think it's gonna change anything."

"But you're the one assigning me a minder. You have the power to walk it back."

Shane shook his head. "No, I don't. They all signed the contract with Rebel PR. The only power I had in all of this was picking Karla as your representative. Karla stays. You know who to call if your knickers are in a twist."

Jack folded his arms across his chest. This was bullshit. He hated the idea of having someone watching his every move. The beautiful Danish woman who turned out was Emil Anderson's bloody sister glared at him with venom in her eyes. At any other time, he'd be delighted. He liked a woman with a bit of spark in her, and Karla Anderson, despite the formal clothing, had it in spades or so Jack believed.

The part of him that was used to driving people away

wondered how much it would take for her to throw the towel in. Like, she was Emil's sister, so he couldn't go full obnoxious prick or else risk falling out with his teammate. Jack couldn't shove her all the way out of Ireland, but he could gently nudge her in the right direction.

Shane glanced at his watch, then at Karla, as if he was done with dealing with Jack. "I have to go and check on a few things with Charlie. You gonna be okay here for a bit?"

"I'm not gonna murder her, Shaney."

Shane rolled his eyes when Jack interjected, but Karla just nodded, though she chewed on her bottom lip like she was nervous.

Shane headed for the door, then looked over at Jack. "Behave, Jack."

Jack gave him a mock salute, ignored the woman watching him, and went about cleaning some of his tools. Although his body was angled away from Karla, he could see her shifting nervously. Jack closed his toolbox, and then leaned against the counter.

He arched his brow as if challenging her to say something and then she did.

"I know this is not something that you wanted, but I assure you that I am good at my job. It will be my responsibility to take control of all the things that interfere with your driving. Feel free to lean on me and offload things that are a distraction."

"I'd have no problem leaning on ya, sweetheart. Preferably naked if that's what you're offering."

Karla folded her arms across her chest, not realizing how much it pushed up her breasts so that they strained against the buttons of her blouse. She gave him an unimpressed look, "I worked with men my entire career, Jack. A little crass talk does not unnerve me. So you can give it your best shot, but I am not going to let you ruin this opportunity for me."

There was a steel in her tone that Jack liked. He would like it even more if she wasn't being paid to be his glorified babysitter.

"Right, so now that we have that out of the way, I have lots of ideas. Luke has a lot of pro LGBTQ sponsorship deals. After what you said about the interview, we could see if we could get them on board. Maybe a sports brand like Eve has. Shane said that a number of clothing brands want a joint photoshoot with you and Luke."

Jack could see the excitement in her eyes, and knew that she had really put some thought into what she wanted to achieve, and she continued to ramble on about plans for exhibitions and showcases. She started to get animated, her hands moving a mile a minute as she paced back and forth in front of him.

Damn, she really was invested in this role.

Jack hated that he was gonna be a prick to her.

Walking over to his car, Jack opened the door, and sat down sideways with his legs on the ground outside. It occurred to him that maybe no one had told her about his disability. If they had, Jack was certain that Karla would have made some suggestion about doing some disability awareness campaign or something.

Jack's lips curved into a smile as a plan formulated in his mind.

Karla had walked over and was continuing to talk as Jack rolled up his right pant leg and began to unclasp his walking leg. Noah had been super supportive when it came to getting his car all kitted out. Jack still had power in his stump. Had worked hard to make it so, and with the special prosthesis that was attached to the accelerator pedal it was almost like normal driving.

The first time that Jack had driven his rally car around the track it had made him cry.

Pushing away those thoughts, Jack waited until Karla came to a stop by the car door, however, she was so animated and excited she didn't even notice anything about Jack.

"Christ, you might not be Irish, but you sure as shit can talk like you've kissed the Blarney Stone. Here, make yourself useful and hold this for me."

With a frown on her face, Karla absently held out her hand and Jack placed his prosthesis in her grasp and waited...

Karla blinked. Jack watched as her eyes slowly shifted down to the prosthesis in her hand and she let out a scream so loud that it made his ears ring. She threw the prosthesis back at him, a look of pure horror on her face, and Jack caught it, laughing so hard his eyes watered.

"Jesus Christ, woman. Don't toss that around like it's not worth a shitton of money."

She stared at him with wide eyes, and Jack held out the prosthesis again, and gave it a little shake.

"Just put that over there on the counter for me, will ya sweetheart?"

"I most certainly will not!" she exclaimed, taking a step back, and Jack bit down on the inside of his mouth so as not to laugh.

Jack hopped out of the car, then hopped over to the counter, brushing past a horrified-looking Karla as he mumbled that he thought she was supposed to make his life easier loud enough for her to hear. Jack wanted to laugh his ass off at how she was staring at his missing limb. He set his walking prosthesis on the counter, just as the door to the garage burst open and Shane came in.

Shane took one look at Karla, then his eyes skirted over to Jack. "We heard screaming."

"He... I....he...."Karla stuttered, her eyes darting from Jack to his prosthesis.

Charlie came in then, concern on her face as she came to stand by Shane. "Is everything okay?"

Karla was shaking her head. "I didn't know. I didn't know."

Shit. Jack wondered if he had broken her. All he had wanted to do was to shock her enough to quit and then Shane would leave him alone. He hadn't wanted to shock her this badly.

But there was no reversing out of it now.

Jack braced himself against the bench. "Listen, I know you said that Karla was here to stay, but I don't think I can work with someone who obviously has an issue with the fact I'm missing a limb."

Shane's gaze narrowed as he looked at Karla. Her mouth opened, then closed, then opened again. Her eyes darted to Jack, as if begging him to say something. Feeling like a complete and utter dickhead, Jack just shrugged.

Her face fell. She looked like she wanted to cry.

Shit, he couldn't handle it when woman cried.

Karla blinked a few times and then she scowled at Jack. "You did that on purpose to freak me out."

"Listen, sweetheart, all I did was ask ya to give me a hand putting my fake leg on the counter while I went and took the car out to see if I fixed the rattle in it. Not my fault if you had a freakout about the fact I'm disabled."

"Jack," Charlie said, taking a step forward and putting her hands on her bump. "I'm sure Karla didn't mean it." She looked at Karla. "Right?"

"I didn't know." Karla said quietly, looking from her employers to Jack. "I didn't know and he just handed it to me and I screamed."

Charlie elbowed Shane. "Oh my god, Shane! Did you not tell her?"

Shane looked a little sheepish. "I forgot."

Jack hopped back over to the car, trying to hide the fact that he was a little bit pleased that Shane hadn't told Karla about his disability, like it was an afterthought and not the main sticking point. He sat down on the seat and leaned forward to rest his elbows on his thighs. "Look it doesn't matter who forgot and all that. She's obviously disgusted. I can see it all over her face. So, nice to meet ya, sweetheart. I'm sure Shaney can find ya some other fully whole sports star to manage and you'll not have to deal with me."

Karla looked like she wanted to argue, but Jack swung himself into his seat, fastened his stump to his driving prosthesis, and hit the start button on the car. The engine roared to life as he yanked the door shut, revved the engine a few times and then peeled out of the garage.

Chapter Eight

Jack

JACK KNEW that being ordered to show up at your PR company's office was not a good thing. He knew that he was in trouble the moment that he had strode in the door to Rebel PR, and Andrea Collins had given him that death stare, pointing at him to sit his ass down and wait. Jack did as he was told, since both Andi and Shane were on a call and his left leg bounced with nervous energy.

To be fair, when he had driven back into the garage and seen that everyone had left, Jack had started to feel guilty. The sheer look of horror on Karla's face when he accused her of being disgusted about his disability had twisted something in his gut. He'd wanted to apologise for being an ass, but two days had passed now, and he hadn't any way of contacting Karla.

He assumed she was gone, and wasn't that what he'd wanted?

Jack leaned forward, his eyes scanning the wall in front of

him that had pictures of all the famous people Rebel PR managed. It was a fucking epic wall to be on, and now he doubted that he'd ever make it up there after what he'd pulled.

This whole thing had a hauled to the principal's office kinda feel.

It wasn't a new sensation to Jack. Before his accident, Jack had always been mischievous, acting up in school to cover up how bad things were at home. Then when he'd eventually gone back to secondary school, minus a limb, Jack had been in the principal's office every couple of days.

Jack slumped in the chair; his arms folded across his chest. The principal was looking at him, expecting him to answer his questions about how Jack had ended up with a split lip, and Edwin had ended up with a missing tooth.

"Jack, you can tell me what happened." Mr. Harrington said to him, giving Jack his best, I'm your friend guise.

Jack arched a brow as if to call bullshit, but still refused to answer his question. He sat there, his lip bleeding and sore, not a word spoken as Jack brimmed with anger.

"Come on, Jack. You have to help me out here. Edwin is telling me that you misheard something he said and just lashed out. I need to hear your side of the story."

Well that sure as shit wasn't going to happen. There was no way he was being a rat and telling Mr. Harrington that Edwin had stuck out his leg and made Jack trip up, hitting his hip off the sharp angle of the desk. Pain was still tearing up his side.

Aww, look lads. The cripple's gonna cry...

That's what the little shit had said and while Edwin had been sparse with the truth. He'd just told Harrington about Jack turning on Edwin and laying into him. Maybe it was being called a cripple, or the class laughing, but Jack had lost it. That word, that horrible fucking word that he had come to hate.

Little cripple boy.

You can't drive in F1 if you're a cripple.

You need to be careful with yourself now that you're a cripple.

If you hadn't of grabbed the wheel, then you wouldn't be a cripple.

"Okay, Jack. I can't force you. You're suspended for a week. Your mother is outside waiting for you."

"Jack?"

Jack blinked away from the memory and looked up to see Shane watching him with a weird expression on his face. Getting to his feet, Jack got his balance, and then followed Shane into Andi's office. Shane took a seat next to Andi, and Andi pointed to the seat at the opposing side of the desk.

Yup – Jack was totally getting his ass handed to him.

"Right, you wanna tell me why you behaved like an immature dickhead?"

Jack reached around and rubbed the back of his neck. "In my defence, I'm an immature dickhead a lot of the time...I think you need to be more specific."

"Don't get smart with me, Jack. I am not in the mood to deal with your flippant sense of humour today. I have a million and one things I need to sort and now trying to persuade a very qualified PR consultant that the client we gave her isn't a massive prick has jumped to the top of my list."

"I - " Jack began, but Andi held up her finger.

"No. I'm not done. And you will stay quiet and listen." Andi paused as if she was daring him to speak but Jack kept his lips firmly clamped shut.

"I don't care if it was laddish banter. I don't care if it was hazing. I. Don't. Care. You are contractually obligated to work with the PR representative that we choose for you. It's a condition of your race contract."

Shit...was that one of the really small, printed terms and conditions that Jack hadn't bothered to look at?

Andi must have seen the look on his face, because she leaned back in her chair. "I called Noah. It's the last thing I wanted to do when he's in full F1 mode. Imagine what that looks like, me calling a world-class athlete because one of his drivers is playing at being a muppet."

Jack winced, squirming in his seat. But he wasn't a fool to speak when Andi was still fuming at him. Jesus, as much as Jack didn't want someone monitoring his every moment, the last thing he wanted was for his behaviour to warrant Andi calling Noah when he was in preseason mode.

"Jack," Shane said with a sigh. "You seem to be under the impression that Karla is going to be a babysitter but that's not what she is in the slightest. I'm certainly not Eve's babysitter. Oskar isn't Quinn's babysitter. Karla is a highly qualified woman who is upset that anyone would think that she was an ableist."

Okay, so Jack had only meant to freak her out a little bit. This was worse than Jack thought.

He didn't want someone handling him though. It made him think of his mam trying to follow him around, trying to make out that he couldn't do things for himself. It was demeaning. He wasn't a cripple, and he didn't want others treating him like that.

"Right, what have you got to say for yourself? And before you get smart and say I'm not your boss, I have full permission of the owners of NLQ Racing to decide what happens after this meeting."

Jack sighed, and ran a hand through his hair. "Did you tell Luke what happened?"

Shane shook his head. "Believe it or not, Karla asked us not to. She said it was an issue with her client and not something that needed to be shared with him. That any decision to stay with Rebel PR would be hers and it was a Rebel PR issue.

You should be grateful for that because as much as you are Luke's teammate, Karla is his family now."

Fuck. He'd been a dickhead and she'd still been professional.

"Look, there's no excuse for what I did. It was a little bit of banter, a little bit of trying to get rid of her."

"Why would you want to get rid of someone whose job it is to not only make us money, but to help you with whatever you need?" Andi asked him.

"You mean like a carer?" Jack replied with a snort. "Cause that's what sticks in my head when you say PA. They tried to give me a PA when I lost me leg, yano. Someone to help me mam to look after me. To wash me. To help me with whatever I needed. They assumed I couldn't do it by myself so instead of giving me the tools to be self-reliant, they wanted me to give in and give up."

"And if you wanna spin things," Jack continued. "I did try and get her to help me by handing over me leg. Not totally my fault she freaked out."

Both Andi and Shane were looking at him, however Jack could see Andi's expression had softened just a little. Shane looked at Andi and then back at Jack before he said. "Maybe I should have prepared Karla more. I genuinely forgot. And no one wants her to be your carer, Jack. Believe me when I say that I went through hundreds of CV's and Karla was the right fit."

Andi glanced at her watch, and sighed, before getting to her feet. "Listen, I have a meeting to go to, so we will wrap this up. While I understand that this might bring up some painful memories, and I'm not unsympathetic, it doesn't change anything. Karla will be your PR Rep from Rebel PR. That's non-negotiable. And let me be clear. If you scare off this talented young woman and we lose her because of your hang-up, then I swear to God, Jack...there will be hell to pay."

With that warning, Andi swept from the office, leaving Jack and Shane sitting there. He waited until the door slammed to the building, and Jack exhaled, feeling like he'd been given a stay of execution.

"Make it right, Jack. Andi is not playing around."

Ya, Jack had got that feeling too.

CHAPTER NINE

Karla

KARLA HAD BEEN ABSOLUTELY livid with Jack O'Neill and herself in equal measures. How dare he pull such a stupid little boy stunt with her and making her look bad! Karla knew that she was normally less reactive to the unpredictable, and was calm under pressure. However, it was not your average day when someone hands you their leg just to unnerve you.

And like a fool, it had done just that.

Of course, Karla should have put all the pieces together when Shane had introduced them. Karla had heard Luke speak of his teammate, a man with a disability who didn't let that stop him, and how it had made Luke feel like he could still be good at rallying, even with the weakness in his hip from his own car accident.

The connection had truly slipped her mind and even when she had been surprised at Jack handing her his prosthetic leg, Karla had been so shocked that she still hadn't pieced it all together until Shane came forward and apologised for not giving her the heads up.

Karla had been trembling with a mixture of shame and fury. She had instantly, out of sheer embarrassment, offered her resignation, telling Shane and Charlie she couldn't work for someone who thought she would be discriminatory toward a client.

Shane and Charlie both had been adamant that they would never think that and persuaded her to wait a few days before making up her mind. She had asked Shane not to tell Luke, even though he was a part owner of the rally team, knowing that Luke would feel compelled to tell Emil, who in turn would rush back to Cork. Emil would want to protect her, like he always had but this was something Karla had to do for herself.

Because what was the point in moving to a new country for a job if she wasn't able to find a way to stand on her own two feet without her brother being by her side? Karla wanted to be independent, strong, doing it for herself ... but knowing that she *could* ask for Emil's help if she needed it.

Karla had spent most of the last couple of days wondering if her mother had been right and that she had indeed made a terrible mistake. She had tried to take her mind off things by sorting her new apartment, going with Luke's mother to get all new bedding and accessories, and then having lunch with the woman.

Perhaps it was an Irish thing, for mothers to be this encouraging, though having seen both of the twin's parents with their children, Karla knew it was mostly the people and a little bit of the culture. Her own mother had yet to answer her calls or call herself.

In fact, it was Lærke who had been the one to send her a present that had made her smile. It was a framed photograph of their little village, blanketed under snow, the stars twinkling in the darkness. It came with a note from Lærke.

Now a little piece of home is with you in your new home.

Fly strong, dear sister. It is time that you had the chance to soar.

Karla had hung the picture over the television, Lærke's note steeling her resolve that she would stay and see this out. Jack might not want to work with her, but he surely needed someone to reign in his lack of filter and impulse control. Karla had taken this morning to look back at previous interviews, and Jack had a massive chip on his shoulder whenever someone brought up his disability or the accident that had led to him losing a limb.

She had also taken the time to read up on the accident and Karla understood Jack a little better after doing her research. She had emailed Shane to ask for Jack's personnel file, had promptly received it delivered to her door with a new work laptop and a note that said that Shane was glad she had decided to stay.

Karla had set up the laptop, then got down to reviewing her client's file. She made notes on Jack, his career, his likes and dislikes, then noted suggestions for sponsorship, campaigns that he might be interested in being the face off and all that.

Shane sent her on details of clothing lines that wanted to get Jack and Luke involved, blushed a little when she read details of the underwear company who were offering an eyewatering sum to get both rally drivers to strip down to their boxers. Emil had once done a similar campaign in Denmark that Karla had never wanted to see but alas, when your brother is on billboards, a sister truly doesn't have a choice.

What would Jack look like in nothing but his boxers?

Karla sat back at that highly inappropriate thought, her cheeks flushing. There was no way that she should even be envisioning Jack almost naked. First of all, he was her client. Second of all, he was rude, inconsiderate, and a PR nightmare most of the time. It did not matter that he was attractive. That was not a line Karla was going to cross no matter how good-looking he was or the seemingly regular occurrence of Rebel PR employees ending up with their clients.

She was not here for any of that. She just wanted to do a good job.

And that did not entail getting romantically involved with a man who was ...what was it Shane had called him... a numpty.

A knock sounded on her door, and Karla closed her laptop to go answer it. Luke Sullivan stood on the other side, smiling at her. His red hair was ruffled in a messy way that Karla knew probably took him some time to do. He wore a Danish team hoodie that was most certainly Emil's. Her brother once told her that Luke wore his hoodie when he was missing him and Karla had taken one look at the goofy look on Emil's face and knew that her brother was smitten.

Luke's lips curved into a smile. "Before you ask, yes, Emil asked me to come check in with you, and yes, I would have come by myself just to see how you coped with shopping with me mam."

Karla laughing, walking back into the apartment with Luke following her. "Your *mam* was such a joy to be around. She took me to all the best places. Helped me pick out some lovely things for the apartment, though I think now I have a standing invitation to Sunday dinners."

"She'll hold ya to that too." Luke said as he lowered himself down on one of the chairs. "She was literally heart-broken when Cathal told her that he'd have to miss some Sundays because when the shop was shut, he already had plans with the Rebel Ink crew. He didn't know what to say when she told him to just bring them all along."

Karla smiled. That did sound like Luke's mother.

They chatted a little about how Emil was doing in the UK, Luke's training plan, how Karla was adjusting to Irish living and adjusting to the weather. Karla made them both coffees, enjoying the company. Her and Luke had not had much time to spend alone since they had been introduced, and it was nice to get to know him on a one-to-one basis.

Luek sipped his coffee, and fiddled with the strings on his hoodie, running his thumb up and down the length.

"You miss him?" Karla asked Luke, and he blushed.

"It's stupid, really, but ya, I do," Luke admitted, setting his mug down on the table. "When I was hiding who I was, I forced myself to pretend that I wasn't missing out on anything. But your brother changed all that. It was weird at first, not sleeping alone. But now, I find it hard to fall asleep when he's not here."

He lifted his gaze to Karla. "See. Stupid."

Karla shook her head, giving him a warm smile. "It is far from stupid. It is rather romantic. I am glad my brother has found someone to love him as much as you do. He gave so much of himself to others, to me, to Lærke, to our parents, even to his country. It was about time the universe gave him something in return."

Luke flushed an even darker shade of red, as Karla laughed and got up to rinse out their cups, giving Luke a moment. She washed out the cups, and left them to drain, as Luke got up and stood on the other side of the breakfast bar.

"So, Charlie and Andi invited a few of us over for dinner. Nothing fancy, since Charlie is about ready to pop and Andi doesn't cook, but they told me to make sure I came and got you."

It was on the tip of her tongue to say no, but Luke insisted. When she sighed, saying she would go, Luke grinned and pulled out his phone. "Brilliant. I'll get Jack to collect us from here then."

Karla's stomach sank but she forced a smile.

This was going to be interesting.

CHAPTER TEN

Jack

WHEN THE INVITE had come through for him to go to Charlie's house for dinner, Jack had been ready to tell Luke that he already had plans. He didn't, but after Andi and Shane chewing him out the other day, he didn't want to make it any more awkward. He still hadn't seen Karla to try and play nice with her, so things all felt uneasy.

He'd also had a little bit of an ache in his tump. Nothing major that he couldn't deal with, but it made him a little cranky. The little bit of pain had kept waking Jack, so he was running on too little sleep and energy drinks.

Considering both Shane and Luke had texted him to come along, Jack had felt like this wasn't an invite that he could turn down. Jack offered to come get Luke, since driving gave him a way to get the hell out of dodge if he wanted to escape.

Jack had not been prepared to get a text from Luke to ask him to come pick him and Karla up at hers. His crankiness was now a full-blown mood as he drove his Subaru into the industrial estate and ground to a halt outside the door of the apartment building Karla was living in.

The music was turned up on full blast, Jack tapping his hands on the steering wheel along to Stereophonics, Dakota, while he pressed the horn on the car and waited. He didn't have to use a special driving prosthetic for driving this car which was something he was always pleased about.

The door to the apartment space opened and Luke stepped out, Karla following after him. Jack turned down the volume on the stereo. He watched as they argued over who would go in the front seat, and Jack could tell that Karla no more wanted to sit beside him than he wanted her to sit in the passenger seat and have to make small talk with her.

In the end, Luke opened the backdoor for her, and Karla slid inside, her eyes lifting to his in the mirror.

"Hello."

"Hey." He replied as Luke got into the passenger seat and held out his fist to Jack.

Jack bumped his fist, then made sure everyone was belted in, then drove off. Luke chatted away to him, oblivious to the obvious tension in the car between him and Karla. Andi had been clear that his contract would be in jeopardy if Karla decided to walk, so Jack felt like he had to play nice.

When there was a lull in Luke's chatter, Jack raised his eyes to the mirror, saw that Karla was watching him right back and his body heated. Fucking stupid thing...it wasn't like she was watching him because she was attracted to him or some shit... was probably just fucking afraid he'd kick off again.

"You settled in?" Jack heard himself say.

"Yes, thank you." Came her polite, yet short reply. Somehow that bugged Jack more than if she had started to chat away like they were besties.

Karla dragged her gaze from his in the mirror and turned to look out the window. Luke glanced at them both, and Jack shrugged his shoulders pretending he had no clue. Luke frowned and Jack concentrated on the road as he drove the short distance to Charlie's house.

Parking the car, Luke hopped out as did Karla, and then Jack slowly got out of the car, ignoring the dart of pain. He must not have hidden it too well, because when he felt the weight of eyes on him, Karla was watching him with a cautious expression.

"You waiting for an escort, sweetheart?" Jack ground out, ashamed that Karla had seen him in pain, and he wanted another reaction from her other than pity. Instead, she rolled her eyes and sauntered off, giving Jack the perfect view of that curvy ass in her jeans.

As she turned to glance over her shoulder, Jack snapped his eyes up just in time, so she didn't see him perving on her. Jack closed the driver's door and locked it, before crossing the gravel and into the house. He closed the front door to the sound of laughter, closed his eyes, and leaned against the door.

His phone rang with the theme song to Jaws, and Jack groaned, ignoring it as he scrubbed his face with his hands.

"You gonna answer that?"

Jack pried open his eyes to see MMA badass Eve Andrews watching him with an amused expression. He'd sparred with Eve a few times in the gym and liked her no BS attitude. Jack shrugged his shoulders, and pushed off the door.

"Maybe you could answer it and tell me Ma that no I haven't fallen off a cliff, or crashed me car, or lost any other vital parts of me body that might put me even more off balance when I take off my prosthetic?"

"Only if you call my mam and tell her that the black eyes and bruised ribs add character and that when a paparazzi snap a photo of me looking like utter shite, it is not a reason to text me pictures of makeup looks that will make my "injuries" less noticeable."

Jack was already laughing when Eve did the air quotes, but now he let loose a chortle of laughter. "Hate to fucking say it, but that totally makes me feel better to know that despite the fact you can kick a grown man's ass, your mam still gives you shit."

Eve threw her eyes up to heaven, then motioned with her head for him to come in. Jack strode into the kitchen, and greeted everyone. Charlie and Andi were arranging some nibbles on the counter, Eve had gone over to where Shane, Luke, and Karla were chatting. For a moment, Jack didn't know where to go, but then Andi called him over and asked him to get some stuff out of the fridge.

Jack busied himself getting stuff from Charlie's really over-stocked fridge. Then he accepted the non-alcoholic beer that Luke handed him, his teammate knowing that Jack never drank and got behind the wheel of a car. Jack knew some people did, but after his dad and all that, Jack had vowed never to do it, to never be his dad.

Jack took a gulp from his bottle, and lifted his eyes to see Karla watching him with a curious expression, then a sympathetic one that grated on him. He tore his eyes away when Luke asked him about something that didn't feel right with his own rally car, and Jack got lost in the conversation.

Despite not wanting to come, Jack enjoyed himself. When Shane and Andi weren't in boss mode, they were a laugh to be around. Charlie was telling them all stories of pranks and things they all used to get up to in Manchester, and even Luke got involved telling them all how Quinn and he had covered Noah's trailer in his first ever modelling campaign because he had hated it.

That had made everyone laugh, including Karla whose laugh made his skin pebble. It was annoying and inconvenient, his attraction to this woman, and it pulled on his patience a little. He didn't have time for the distraction and working every day with Karla would be one hell of a distraction.

He glanced at Luke, who was wearing his boyfriend's hoodie, and wondered what Karla would look like wearing one of his?

Fucking hell, he needed to either get laid, or at least do something to get her out of his head. At first, Jack had wanted her gone because he didn't want to have a minder following after him, making him do shit he didn't want to do, but now, he realized that he was thinking about her more and more and that wasn't gonna happen here.

He wasn't a relationship kinda guy and Emil would kill him if he fucked and ducked his little sister...

Fuck...now he was imagining Karla naked and that was not where he needed his thoughts to go.

Pain flared in his leg and Jack tried to walk as casually as possible over to one of the chairs and he sat down, wishing he could just take off his prosthetic and sit there freely. He didn't feel comfortable enough yet around everyone to just do it like he would at home, or even at the garage, so Jack just bit back the ache, and drank his non-alcoholic beer.

His mam had been on at him for years to go back to how he was before the accident, when he had friends and went and did things other than racing. His mam didn't realize that Jack had only pretended to go out with friends when he'd actually been at the race track.

Jack hadn't needed friends...he had racing.

Every spare minute he had was to work toward getting that F1 drive. He hadn't had any time for friends when his dream was within reach. Philip had promised him...

And then his Da had taken it all away.

Maybe having friends wasn't all that bad...

Maybe this time, he could have his career and some friends.

CHAPTER ELEVEN

Karla

EVERYONE WAS TALKING about the times their shared pasts and Karla felt a little like the odd one out. Even Jack managed to interact with them seamlessly. Perhaps Luke had only invited her because she was Emil's sister. Maybe Charlie and Andi had invited her to their gathering because of what had happened with and they were making sure she stayed.

Back in Denmark, Karla had few friends from college that she was still in contact with, but Emil and Lærke, and Oskar, since he and Emil were inseparable. She wanted to make friends in Ireland. She wanted to get on with her colleagues. Maybe it was just a little bit of homesickness, or maybe it was that Karla was still questioning her decision.

She looked around, hoping to catch Luke's eye, but instead, her eyes landed on Jack. He looked just as uncomfortable as she did. Karla was reminded of the sharp look of pain that had flashed across his face when he had gotten out of the car, and then the equally sharp response to him finding Karla had been watching him.

Jack must have sensed her eyes on him because he lifted his gaze to hers. He stared at her, his gaze narrowing. Then he crooked his finger and beckoned her over.

Karla didn't want to go when he summoned her like that. She dug her heels in, not taking her eyes off him as he sighed, shrugged, and went back to drinking his non-alcoholic beer as if he didn't care if she came over or not.

With a sigh, Karla strode over to where Jack was lounging in his seat, folded her arms across her chest, and arched her brow as if to say what do you want.

Jack's lips curved into a cheeky smile. "You having a good time?"

Karla blinked in surprise, not expecting Jack to be sincere to her. "I am." She replied, allowing herself to smile back at Jack.

"Then you should tell your face that cause you look miserable as fuck."

"I do not!" Karla exclaimed, frowning at the man who was now smirking at her.

"Well, maybe give the resting bitch face a night off and grin and bare it like everyone else."

"You are an awful person!" Karla told him, and the numpty laughed, and lifted his bottle as if to cheers her comment. Karla wished she had never come over to talk to him.

"Glad you understand that, sweetheart." Jack said with a grin. "Now it might stop you from running to your bosses because you can't take a joke. If you plan on hanging round in Ireland, you'll have to understand that we have a tendency to banter and take the piss."

How dare he? Arrrrgh, Jack was just so infuriating.

"Well, you should try being a nicer person, Jack. One thing you will learn about me is that I am very stubborn, and all of your silly little antics will not scare me off. So, perhaps you should suck it up and try and behave like a civilized human being and stop behaving like a numpty."

"I love a challenge, sweetheart. And I can out stubborn you. If you looked up stubborn in the dictionary, you'd see my handsome face looking back at you."

Karla snorted, rolling her eyes. "I'm sure it would be, sat right next to the words obnoxious, annoying, conceited, and probably asshole too!"

Karla didn't realize how loud her voice had gotten but she could see everyone looking at them in the reflection in the patio door. She suddenly felt self-conscious, and was about to try and walk it back, but that was exactly what Jack wanted. If she backed down now, he would see it as a victory and there was no bloody way that Karla was going to let him win.

They were glaring at each other, her and Jack, his eyes were hot and fierce. Her mouth was suddenly dry, her lips too. Karla licked her lips and felt a secret thrill as Jack's lips shifted to track the movement, then back up to her eyes with added heat.

A dark laugh sounded behind her, and then she heard Shane's girlfriend Eve say. "Oh ya, I'm calling it now. Those two are gonna be fucking each other's brains out before we all know it."

Heat burned her cheeks. She was appalled at the urge to either yank Jack to his feet and kiss him, or crawl into his lap and do the same. He was angry, she could feel it, and Karla couldn't help but wonder if Jack would fuck her in anger.

What the hell was wrong with her?

As if he was thinking the same thing, Jack growled, and surged to his feet. Karla wondered for a moment if he was going to kiss her, here, in front of all these people. She watched as the heat left his eyes, replaced with a lick of pain as he stumbled.

On instinct, Karla reached out to prevent him from falling and Jack jerked back as if she had been about strike him. It didn't stop Karla from noticing that he almost stumbled at his retreat too.

"I fucking got it."

Karla could tell from his tone that he was embarrassed. Could see it in the way he ducked his gaze. Something about it all made him seem vulnerable, young even, and Karla wanted to put a reassuring hand on his arm to offer him some comfort.

But something told her that Jack wouldn't welcome any comfort from anyone, not just her.

"Jack," Shane started to say as he walked over.

A fake smile curved Jack's lips. "I'm grand, Shaney. Had too much to drink, eh? Charlie, Andi, thanks for the hospitality, great shindig and all but I'm gonna shoot off. Luke, mate, I'm sure you can sort out a lift home."

Jack brushed past Karla, not sparing her a second glance as he walked over to the counter, put his bottle down, and as Karla turned around, she saw him tip an imaginary hat and stride out the door. Eve looked around the room, then jogged out after Jack.

Luke came over and asked if Karla was all right and what the hell was going on. Karla shook her head, unable to tell Luke all of it, and heard Andi explain to Luke about the incident the other day. She heard the front door open, as the unmistakable roar of an engine and the thump, thump of a stereo before the peel of tyres sounded, and then nothing.

Eve came back in and shook her head when Shane asked was Jack okay.

Luke looked at her, and put his hand on her arm. "Why didn't you tell me that Jack was being a dick to you?"

Karla sighed, shaking her head. "Because you would have

told Emil, and he would come rushing in to try and save the day. I can handle it. I can handle Jack and I didn't need Emil coming to my rescue and making me look incompetent in front of my new bosses, just like you are doing now."

Understanding flickered in Luke's eyes and he nodded after a moment. "I won't tell Emil. And I'm sure Jack being a dickhead only proves to everyone that he is a dickhead and has nothing to do with how capable you are of doing the job."

Charlie came over, one hand on her bump, a reassuring smile on her face. "One hundred percent what Luke said. This does not take from any of the reasons why we chose you for Rebel PR. Jack obviously has a stick up his ass and an *I am man* complex that he needs to get over."

"Hey." Shane and Luke said in unison and Eve burst out laughing.

"Present company excluded," Charlie said with a grin. "The moral of this is don't be worried. We support you all the way and if Jack needs another talking to, then we can all do it. And if he is still being a git, I'll give him a swift kick up the ass or put him on a timeout."

Andi barked out a laugh. "And they tell me that you are the nice one and I'm the dictator."

"I've been binge-watching Supernanny."

Karla laughed with them, worry still gnawing at her stomach but she shoved it aside and let herself enjoy the company and the conversation. Now that Jack wasn't here to draw her attention, Karla relaxed a little more, and everyone was very welcoming.

She was surprised when Eve told her that she was going to be doing some sessions with some of the other women in their friend circle at the gym, and that Karla should come along. Eve leaned into Shane and grinned. "Mostly, we bitch about men, and paparazzi, and stupid judgemental people so come along, and we can all imagine we are punching Jack and it will make you feel so fucking better."

That had Karla looking at Eve with a shocked expression, as Shane rolled his eyes and kissed Eve's cheek, and said. "Ruthless, isn't she? You should try taking a punch from her. That's when she stole my heart."

CHAPTER TWELVE

Jack

"You need to get out of bed, Jack."

Like fuck he did. He didn't want to get out of bed to take a piss, or a shower, or any of the fucking rehab training they wanted him to do. He sure as shit did not want to get out of bed to be fitted for the fake leg they were trying to palm off on him.

"It's an important step in your recovery. Come on now. doctor's orders."

Jack looked at the nurse beaming at him from the end of his bed, cocked his eyebrow. "Well, just like I told ya last time, you can tell the doctor to shove his stethoscope right up his-"

"Jack O'Neill, do not finish that sentence."

Jack turned his glare over to his ma. She'd been on his case too. It had been weeks since they had chopped off his leg. Weeks since his dad had died, and his little sister gone before she'd even had time to breathe. His dream of driving an F1 car was over. Every shitty thing that Jack had been forced to live through to get to where he wanted to be now seemed like an utter waste of time.

What was the fucking point of any of it anymore?

What was the point of being alive?

"I think Jack might be a little depressed."

Jack rolled his eyes at his mother. "Maybe we should chop off your leg and see if you are all sunshine and fucking rainbows, Ma."

"Watch your language, Jack." Ma snapped at me, shattering the doting mam persona she'd been trying to portray when she had finally found it in her to rock up to the hospital.

Jack snorted, shifting in the bed. He hated being stuck here, looking at all the bland white walls, the positive quotes about rising to the challenge, looking to the future, and all that fucking bullshit. The doctor told him that to get out of this place, he had to commit to the rehab, to making a positive step toward a recovery.

But Jack was angry. Angry at his da for dying and getting away with all the horrible shit he had done. He died and left chaos in his wake and Jack wasn't even sad that the asshole was dead. He cared only for the fact that he'd never be able to forget the fact that his da had ruined his body, and in doing so, had left Jack with a permanent reminder of what an asshole his da was.

A knock sounded on the door and Jack lifted his gaze to see a girl around his age standing in the doorway. She had strawberry blond hair, freckles across her nose and cheeks, and a cheery smile. She also had two wicked-looking blades attached to her stumps.

"Hi, I'm Ashling. A few of us are gonna play basketball in the gym later on. Did you want to join us?"

The girl, Ashling, looked around the room and frowned. "Oh, have you not got your prosthesis yet? It doesn't matter. Chris in 5B uses a wheelchair and he usually kicks our ass with his throw. He's like a speed demon in his chair."

Jack hated how sunshiny she sounded. This Ashling sounding optimistic and fun, and well-adjusted with her cool running blades and he was still in bed, wallowing. She gave Jack a smile like she and Jack shared a secret.

"Isn't that nice, Jack? We could get the doctor to get you a wheelchair and you could hang out with some of the other teenagers."

"We can certainly arrange that Jack." The nurse said and everyone was smiling at him with a sickening sweetness that made Jack want to throw something at them.

"No." Jack ground out, his chest heavy. His vision blurred, and he sure as shit didn't want to cry in front of some girl.

"Come on, Jack. It will do you good to get out of this room." His Ma told him, like a pretty girl and some disabled friends would help him get over it.

"I said no," Jack yelled, turning to face his Ma. He didn't know if the girl was still standing in the doorway, and he really didn't care. "I don't want to sit in a wheelchair and pretend that this is my new normal."

"Jack..."

"No, ma. Sitting in a wheelchair makes this real and I'm not ready for this to be real. I do not accept this. I can't accept this. So fuck off with your positivity shit and leave me alone. I wish I'd died in that fucking car wreck. I wish that bastard had killed me too!"

His Ma jerked back like Jack had struck her. "You don't mean that."

Jack laughed shaking his head. "I do. I really fucking do and if I cared enough to get out of this fucking bed, I'd throw myself out the fucking window and be done with it all."

"Oh Jack."

"Get out!" Jack screamed at his ma. "Get the fuck out and leave me the hell alone!"

His Ma didn't budge, and Jack shoved at the monitor next to him. It crashed to the ground, and Jack grabbed the stupid hospital table and tried to topple it over. He misjudged his balance and as the table tipped over, so did Jack. He landed on the floor awkwardly, pain shooting up his leg but there was no leg to feel the pain.

"Oh Jack, let me help you."

"Don't touch me! I got it. Just leave me alone, Ma."

Jack tried to get to his feet, then remembered that he didn't know how to get up now that he only had one working leg. Shame and embarrassment washed over him, and Jack managed to pull himself into a sitting position and leaned against the wall.

He hated this. He fucking hated this.

Jack put his head in his hands and sobbed.

Jack lurched awake in the bed, searing pain shooting up and down his leg. Tossing the duvet aside, Jack screamed at the iron-hot pain that threatened to make him vomit all over the floor. Jack focused on where the pain was coming from and tried to focus on something other than the pain.

This pain was not something Jack was unfamiliar with. Not only had he lost his limb, but he'd also been given the gift of Phantom limb pain. That meant that sometimes, his brain forgot that the limb wasn't there anymore and liked to give Jack mind-numbing pain every once in a while.

Pain scorched him again, and Jack swore, reaching for the mirror that he kept stashed beside the bed. He placed it beside his intact limb and focused on the image in the mirror. When he'd first been given the mirror therapy intervention method, Jack had been skeptical, but over the years, it had helped him.

The pain started to subside, and Jack leaned against his headboard. He should have known that what happened at Charlie's house the other night would bring up some awful memories for him. He might pretend that he was well adjusted and had overcome his amputation to be better than he was before, but there was a part of Jack that still hated his Da for what he had done and hated that everything was harder for him now.

Karla's face when he had stumbled, how she had reached for him with a concerned look on her face, Jack hated that. Would she see him as less of a man? Would she see him as less of an athlete now that she had seen him be weak?

Why the fuck did it bother him so damn much?

Knowing that he'd not get back to sleep now, Jack put his mirror back where he kept it, and grabbed his crutch. He felt a sharp sting in his stump, and hesitated before grabbing some of his anti-inflammatory gel and rubbing it in. He'd give his doctor a call sometime in the next few days, just to make sure everything was grand.

Jack used the crutch and made his way to the kitchen, making himself some eggs and toast, and a coffee, before sitting down with it by the window. It wasn't yet really morning, the sun still yet to rise, but Jack liked this time in the morning, it was peaceful and calm, not tainted by the day.

His head felt full, like all the hateful things he felt about himself were trying to come to the forefront of his mind. It would be grand though, he just needed to work out and clear his head and focus on something other than the shit in his head.

There would probably be no one at the gym this morning, so he could sweat out his demons, and try and make sense of things. If nothing else he could work himself to exhaustion and hope it drowned out his nightmares.

Jack threw on some workout clothes, and attached his prosthetic, ignoring the hiss of pain. It would be grand, sure it would...it would all be grand.

CHAPTER THIRTEEN

Karla

KARLA HAD THROWN herself into work first thing Monday morning. After the gathering at Charlie's house, Karla had felt a little better about her choices and wasn't going to worry about the fact that Jack obviously didn't like her. The truth was Jack didn't have to like her. This was her job, and Shane and Andi, and Charlie all had faith in her, and Karla wanted to be positive and prove herself to them.

As Luke dropped her off in the taxi after Jack had bailed, Karla had begged him not to tell Emil because she wanted to handle this herself. Luke had looked like he didn't want to keep this from Emil, however, Karla explained that she was trying to prove to herself that she could do it without needing Emil's help.

But also being safe in the knowledge that if it all got too much, Karla could go to her brother.

Luke smiled as the taxi pulled up outside her place and gave her a little nudge. "Jack can be a cheeky git sometimes, and I know it doesn't seem like it but he's a good guy. He just hasn't had many friends. Believe it or not, Noah was the same when I met him. It took ages to get him to crack a smile, or even agree to eat with me."

Karla snorted. "I doubt Jack wants to be in the same room as me, let alone eat a meal."

"I can have a word. Tell him to back off."

"Luke," Karla replied with a soft smile, knowing that Luke was being protective of her like she was already family. "Thank you, but I need to handle it myself. If I have my brother-in-law fighting my battles for me, then I will never gain Jack's respect."

"Brother-in-law?" Luke said with a surprised expression, his cheeks flushed.

Karla leaned over and kissed his cheek. "Of course. It is only a mere formality. It will be official, I think, one day."

Karla had left Luke in the car and gone inside and slept better than she had in days. It had motivated her to dive in and worry less about how Jack O'Neill felt about her and more about how damn good she was going to be at this job.

It also gave Karla time to read up on her client. Jack O'Neill was twenty-four years old who was once tipped to be a future F1 world champion. He had won karting title after karting title, so much so that Charlie's father, Philip Coyle had signed him up to Rebel Racers with the idea to put him in a car as soon as a seat became available. There was even chatter that Philip was thinking of volleying to get him in the junior teams in F2 or F3.

Then the career that Jack had dreamt of was stripped away so cruelly.

He was involved in a car accident that had killed his father and unborn sister. That little detail had made Karla's heart hurt. Jack had been pinned in the car and the only way to extract him from the car was to cut the car apart, such was the damage.

Jack almost bled out on the way to the hospital and to save

his life, his right leg from the knee down had been amputated. He'd been in hospital for almost two years, rehabbing and learning to adjust. All of this was in his personnel file, which Rebel PR had filled extensively with medical tests, history, and even a psychiatric report.

Karla had not wanted to read anything too personal, but she couldn't help herself. It was, as she had suspected. Jack had unresolved anger toward his father. Apparently, Jack's father had been a drunk, and he had gotten behind the wheel of his car with his son, and pregnant wife and crashed into a wall.

Jack had not accepted his limb loss well. He'd been distant and reluctant to begin his PT. He had, even at fourteen, banned his mother from his hospital bed and refused to engage with anyone. It had taken months before he could even look at his stump without succumbing to rage.

And then one day it was like a switch had flipped. He started his rehabilitation. He had worked out and out in the effort. He was determined, motivated, and pig headed, which Karla could believe. He had still kept himself separate from other teens but had made positive steps in his recovery.

Karla pushed thoughts of what she had read about Jack away as she worked through the email list that Shane had cc'd her in, and filtered out the ones that she believed Jack might consider. She filtered through them, adding them to different folders for yes, no, and maybes.

The door to Rebel PR opened and Shane came in, talking on his phone. He lifted his hand in greeting, walked into his office, and paced around the rectangular glass. He was talking very animatedly, and then he rolled his eyes, before striding out of the office.

"Collins, relax. I've got it covered. Let the rockstar wine and dine you for a couple of days. The place won't fall apart."

Andi must have said something that had Shane rolling his eyes. "I'm good, Collins. And Eve is around for a couple of days before she heads back. Once you are back before the weekend, so I don't have Ronan pouting at me for breaking our plans, we're good. Besides, Karla has put a serious dent in the NLQ Racing emails. So go and make goo-goo eyes at your rockstar or I'll sic Charlie on ya."

Shane barked out a laugh and hung up the phone. Eve had told Karla the other night that Shane used to be a gymnast, and that he'd been in a really bad place a while ago, however, he was making very good progress. Karla hadn't wanted to pry, and Eve didn't elaborate, but something told Karla that it was something to see Shane laughing and looking carefree.

He slid his phone into his pocket and came over by Karla's desk, hopped up on the free desk. "Declan dragged Andi off for a few days to rest. She has control issues, does Collins. But she needed downtime. Dec is the only person who could force her to do it."

"I can take on more responsibility if it helps Andi with her workload."

Shane smiled, folding his arms across his chest. "Funny you should say that 'cause I need a favour."

Karla sat back in her chair and arched a brow, and that made Shane laugh.

"I promise it's nothing nefarious," Shane reassured her. "Noah managed to talk some fella who owns a woodland in the UK that some of the rally drivers use for practice into letting Luke and Jack have it to themselves for two whole days in a couple of weeks."

"That will be great for them both. But what is the favour?" Karla asked.

"I need someone to act as Rebel PR's representative. The cars will be brought over on the ferry, and I think Jack will probably drive his own car instead of letting someone else drive. So, will you go with them and make sure everything runs smoothly?"

This was a major opportunity for Karla and Shane was putting a lot of trust in her so early in her career with Rebel PR. The thought of being stuck with Jack for a few days wasn't ideal, but Karla wouldn't let this opportunity pass her by.

"I can see you thinking, and we all trust you to do this. And if that doesn't entice you, then I have managed to secure a box to see your brother play when his team goes against Manchester United before ye come home."

It had been a while since she had seen Emil play for his premier league team, and it would be great to see Emil when he wasn't due back to Cork for another couple of weeks. And she had worked with enough footballers to know that even if Emil was not playing for the home side, being in the Theatre of Dreams was something special.

"I can go, if you don't want to." Shane broached.

Karla shook her head. "No, I can go. Just tell me what you need me to organize, and I'll do it."

Shane grinned, then told her that he would sort the transfer of the cars to the UK, if she could call Luke and ask if he what they needed to arrange to be put on the transporter, like his helmet, racer suit, and all that. Then Karla double-checked Jack's phone number with Shane so she could ask him the same.

"Head in next door, the headcase has been working out since early hours. He looked lost in thought when I popped my head in."

Shane's phone rang then, as Karla got to her feet. She grabbed her own phone, steeled her resolve, and ignored the fluttering nerves in the pit of her stomach. Here's hoping that this interaction wouldn't result in another argument.

Chapter Fourteen

Karla

KARLA WAS NOT ashamed to admit that it took her a few minutes to steel her resolve and stride into the gym. The steady thrum of music greeted her when she made her way inside, looking past the boxing ring and to the training area toward the back of the room. Her eyes scanned the room, landing on a half-naked and very sweaty Jack.

His back was to her as he pulled himself up and then down on a bar that was attached between two pillars. His biceps and triceps flexed as he moved, as did the muscles on his back and Karla had never known that back muscles could be so damn sexy.

Jack's grey shorts hung low on slim hips, and she kinda sort of wished he was facing her so she could get a glimpse of what she knew must be a finely sculpted physic. Sweat dripped down from his hair, caressing his spine in a way that made Karla's thighs clench together.

Feeling like an utter fool for being attracted to this man who hated her but she found him strangely intriguing, Karla took a few steps in Jack's direction, then noticed that his prosthesis was set carefully to the side and he was wearing none.

As if he sensed her eyes on him, Jack glanced over his shoulder, his gaze narrowed. Karla prepared for him to have a go at her, but she watched as he hung from the bar with one hand and pressed the sports watch on his wrist to turn off the music.

The strength in his arms must be significant to be able to balance to do that.

It did not do anything to put a halt to the ache between her legs.

"If I didn't know any better, I'd think you were checking out my ass."

Karla snorted, rolling her eyes, trying to stop her face from heating, because as much as she hadn't been checking out his ass, Karla had been checking him out. "You should be so lucky."

A grin curved his lips, and Karla wondered if Jack knew that it changed his face and made her watch to press her lips to his so she could feel that smile against her mouth. Karla watched as Jack turned on the bar to face her, that misleading charming smile remaining on his face as he shifted his weight and then dropped down.

Every instinct in Karla urged her to rush forward to catch him should he falter, but she stayed locked in place as Jack landed with catlike reflexes, balancing on one foot as he grabbed a towel and proceeded to wipe the sweat from his face, then his torso.

His very nice, well-defined torso.

Karla was suddenly very jealous of the towel.

Jack arched a brow as he saw her eyes dip, and she brought them up to his face so fast Karla was surprised she didn't do herself an injury. He hopped on one foot to the nearby bench and sat down, pulling on a tee, and covering a body that Karla was having trouble not looking at.

He took a water bottle out of his bag, took a long drink, then leaned back on the bench.

"Did ya need something?"

Oh right...Karla was actually here for a reason...

"Shane asked me to accompany you and Luke to the UK when you both go for some test-driving. He is sorting travel details for the cars, but if you give me a list of things you need, helmet, race suit, and that, I can make sure they are all on the transporter."

Jack frowned and Karla wished he would go back to smiling. "I can sort all that."

Karla held back her sigh and shrugged. "It is literally part of my job. If you want to get them together and give them to me, then that is fine too. I'm there to make sure you and Luke have nothing else to worry about but getting some laps in. Is it laps when it's rallying?"

The smile returned, making Karla's stomach flip. "It's a stage just so ya know. We'll have to get ya like a rally terminology dictionary or something."

"Listen," Karla started after a heartbeat of silence. "I know that you are unhappy that I've been hired to do your PR and that, and you dislike me because of it, however, I really am here to make it so that you can focus on driving and don't have to deal with as Luke calls it, political bullshit. We can have an amicable work relationship."

Jack ran his fingers through his hair, giving it a mussed look that made Karla think about what Jack would look like just after walking up. She shook her head, as Jack reached for his prosthesis, and began to strap it on. He did so with his eyes on her, and she wasn't sure if she should look away to give him the privacy or keep looking at him as if he were testing her reaction.

In the end, Karla kept her eyes on him, and when Jack had attached his prosthetic, Karla sat down on the bench beside him. Jack's eyes roamed over her, assessing her but Karla wasn't easily unnerved.

"It must have taken a strong will to relearn how to do everyday tasks after the accident."

It was a statement, rather than a question, but Jack barked out a laugh, making Karla smile. "Not sure about that now. Me Ma would say it was sheer stubbornness."

"Perhaps a little bit of both then?" Karla ventured, earning a look from Jack, but his lips were curved.

"I deserved that. I've been a bastard to ya." Jack said as he rubbed a hand up and down his thigh. "Listen, I'm not good with change. Never have been. And I hate thinking that you've been hired to babysit me. I can do shit by myself and just 'cause I have a disability doesn't mean I need help all the time."

Karla shook her head. "I am not here to play your nursemaid, Jack. I am here in a professional capacity to handle media and any other related issues. Noah and Quinn both have race managers. Eve has Shane. Andi handles all of JJ, Ronan, Oli, and Danika's day-to-day stuff. I am sorry if this makes you uncomfortable, but I must tell you that I am not here to stroke your ego or babysit you. That is, what is the phrase? Below my pay grade."

Jack was quiet for a while, then he grabbed a hoodie and pulled it over his head, tousling his hair even more. His intense green eyes watched her, then his shoulders sagged and though his tone wasn't exactly friendly, it wasn't hostile either.

"Since it looks like you aren't going anywhere, I'll try and be civil."

"I would be so grateful," Karla said, not bothering to hide the sarcasm in her tone.

"And this doesn't make us friends."

This time Karla snorted and rolled her eyes. "Perish the thought."

With a growl, Jack got to his feet and picked up his bag. "Jaysus, you're gonna fucking drive me crazy, aren't ya?"

Karla shrugged and got to her feet, folding her arms across her chest. "I'll try not to. You'll get me that list when you have a moment?"

Jack frowned, then held out his hand, making a gimmie motion. "Gimmie your phone."

Karla reached into the pocket of her jeans, and then handed Jack her phone after unlocking it. He tapped away, finding his phone number and then his phone rang, having called it from her phone. "I've got your number now, so I'll message ya."

"Thank you," Karla said, taking her phone as he handed it back to her.

"Sure, whatever," Jack said before turning and heading out of the gym, leaving her standing there unsure of what to make to the most civilized conversation they had shared since she arrived in Cork. To be honest, she suspected that this pleasant Jack wasn't going to stick around for long and he would revert back to being difficult to deal with.

This was something Karla would just have to get used to. She had been truthful with him about not being here to play his nursemaid, and yet, she had peeled back a layer of the hostility and was a little bit closer to understanding everything that made Jack O'Neill tick.

Karla had always loved solving puzzles, and Jack O'Neill was the biggest puzzle she had ever come across. She had spent a ridiculous amount of time trying to figure him out and now, getting to spend more time with him, Karla would get the chance to study him more.

Her phone pinged and she glanced at the message to see that it was from Jack. She felt a pang of excitement, then opened the message and almost growled in frustration at the contents of the message.

Smokey Bacon Taytos - the proper ones.

Barrys Teabags.

Dairygold butter.

Denny Sausages.

Jack had sent her a shopping list. Guess he was done playing nice.

Chapter Fifteen

Jack

Just because Jack and Karla had forged an uneasy truce didn't mean Jack was gonna take it easy on her. The last week getting ready to head to the UK had been a flurry of packing, getting fitted for an updated race suit, and taking delivery of a helmet that Noah had designed for him. He'd been up at Rebel Racers when Luke came in with the two bags, one for Jack and one for Luke.

Luke's helmet was an homage to his Rebel Racers days, in a red and white with a little Danish on it that Luke said meant something like courage is when you fall down and get back up. It suited Luke considering that he had almost been killed in the sport he loved and had to accept that he had a new purpose in life.

Jack had turned his own helmet over, admiring the chequered flag design that had all the dates of the karting competitions that he had won, as well as a phoenix design with graffiti writing that said from the ashes...

Noah Donovan knew how to design a helmet.

78

Jack had made a point of organizing all his stuff and putting them to one side, sending a picture to Karla to tell her that he had all his things together. Jack had tapped his foot on the ground as he waited for a reply, only to get just a second before she had come striding into the garage.

"What are you doing here?"

Karla rolled her eyes as Luke elbowed him, making Jack glare at his teammate. "What?"

Luke sighed. "Be nice."

"I was."

Luke shook his head as he hugged Karla, then ushered her over to where Luke had put his things that needed to go in the transporter. Jack waited impatiently, frowning as he looked at the beautiful woman. She was dressed casually, more casual than Jack had ever seen her and he liked this side of her.

Skintight jeans hugged her curves, and she wore a Denmark team hoodie. Her hair hung loose around her shoulders and when she laughed at something Luke said, the hairs on his arms stood to attention. His reaction to her was starting to annoy him even more than having her as his manager.

As if she felt his eyes on her, Karla looked over her shoulder and said something to Luke before she strode over and leaned against the counter. "Is that everything?"

"I'm sure I'll find something else in the next couple of days."

Karla gave him a look that said she knew that he would but then Jack grinned. "Did ya get the stuff for my rider?"

Karla tilted her head, and gave him a sassy smile that Jack knew she was probably cursing him inside her head even as she said. "Of course. Luke also gave me a list, so I killed two birds with one shopping trip. Please don't hesitate to let me know if there is anything else before Friday."

Jack wanted to rattle her. He really wanted to know what he could do to unsettle her because right now, she looked pretty settled and enjoying the fact that his little demands were not riling her up in the slightest.

Maybe he'd kill her and see if that did it?

Fuck, that was not a path he wanted his thoughts to travel on because Jack had spent too much fucking time wondering what she'd look like, naked, in his bed, his hands on that smooth skin of hers.

Karla must have said something to him, but he'd missed it thinking about her naked.

"I'm sorry, what?" Jack blinked to try and put a curb to his lustful thoughts as Luke came over and slung an arm around Karla's shoulder.

"She asked if you wanted to join us for dinner. Luna and the band are heading off in a few days, so we are going for something to eat, a few drinks, and just hang out. You fancy it?"

Jack knew that he should say yes, try and be a functioning member of society, and try and socialize but the thought of making small talk with strangers and being stuck with the woman who haunted his thoughts for a couple of hours sounded like a slow torture.

Rubbing the back of his neck, Jack replied. "Thanks, but I told me Ma I'd stop by before we head off next week. Next time."

Luke had given him a yeah right expression before his phone rang and he went outside of the garage to answer it. Karla was looking at him, one of her brows arched.

"What?" Jack asked, his voice almost a snarl.

"It might do you good to have some friends. Luke is a really nice guy, and he just wants to be your friend. You should let him."

Jack ran a hand through his hair. Luke and his previous teammates had this great relationship, which had become like family, and Jack knew that Luke was trying to recreate that with him and that Jack was being an asshole to the man.

But he wasn't about to let Karla get one over on him.

"I'm not lying." He told her. "I did tell me Ma that I'd go see her."

Karla shrugged, then glanced over her shoulder to check Luke wasn't coming back in. "Okay, sure. It can't be fun just working out and driving. Everyone is really nice. You might actually have a good time, but maybe that's what you are afraid of..."

Her voice had trailed off then as Luke came back in and asked Karla if she was ready to go. Jack said goodbye to Luke, and inclined his head to Karla, then the two vanished to the sound of Karla's laughter, leaving Jack standing by himself in the garage.

He hadn't gone to see his Ma. Nope, like the saddo he was, Jack locked up the garage, drove home, cooked himself some food, then plonked down to watch a couple of episodes of some show on Netflix.

Jack had then proceeded to jump on his socials, then went total stalker and checked out Luke and Luna's socials. There had been a few photos uploaded, and he scanned them for any pictures of Karla, and found one of her smiling at Rhys Collins, Andi's younger brother.

Jealously had speared through Jack, though he knew it was completely unwarranted because Rhys and his girlfriend Shay had been together for over a year and were totally committed to each other. But it was Karla, smiling in such a friendly way that Jack never got that made him jealous.

Pathetic ...considering that the way he acted toward Karla didn't warrant a smile like that.

It was the night before they were due to travel to the UK and Jack couldn't sleep. He'd gotten a text from Karla asking if he was all set for the morning, and he'd messaged back that he was. He'd spent a ridiculous amount of time trying to come up with a witty response only to find that he didn't have it in him tonight to be snarky with her.

Jack finished packing his clothes, and put the gear bag on the couch before he felt a twinge in his stump. Sitting down, Jack unhooked his prosthetic, setting it aside as he rolled off the sock. Looking down at his stump, he could see that it was inflamed, and it felt sore to touch.

He'd been fitted for a new driving prosthetic, and it still needed a few adjustments, but they hadn't time to get it all done for the testing so Jack had told them that he'd give it a go and they could tweak the fit once he got back. A week of using it and he'd aggravated the skin around where his leg had been amputated.

Knowing that he should call his doctor, and get some antibiotics to stave off any infection, Jack lied to himself that it would be grand till he got home in a few days. He got some of his moisturizer for his skin, lashed it on, and sat and let it dry in, ignoring the slight sting as he focused on the next few days.

It surprised Jack when he picked up his phone and sent Karla a message, asking her if she needed to be collected in the morning. Since he was driving his car over on the ferry, Luke and Karla were gonna travel with him. Jack hated flying, because he had to have his prosthetic on full display for security, and he always felt self-conscious.

Karla had come back to say she was going to book a taxi to go to Luke's, so Jack just told her he would collect her on the way to Luke's no hassle. Her response back was polite, and Jack could tell she was surprised by his offer because all she said was okay, thank you.

The next couple of days were meant to be fun, and while Jack was looking forward to tearing around the forest and really getting a feel for the car, he also had to spend it playing nice with both Luke and Karla, which meant dinners and hell, even a football game.

This was gonna be a long week.

Chapter Sixteen

Karla

KARLA HAD NOT BEEN EXPECTING Jack to offer to collect her before picking up Luke. Nor was she expecting the car journey and the boat ride over to be as much fun as it had been. They had an area reserved next to a window and Karla had perched herself on the window ledge to look out at the water. Luke and Jack had pulled out a laptop and were playing a driving game and trash-talking one another.

Jack had been civil, even friendly, checking in with her to see if she needed anything. She might have thought that she'd imagined it, if not for the slightly amused expression on Luke's face as he looked from Jack to Karla when Jack brought her down a hot chocolate.

Luke had fallen asleep on one of the chairs halfway through the afternoon, and Jack had buried his face in some handwritten notes and Karla stretched herself out to answer some emails. She had glanced at Jack a couple of times, saw him rub at his knee a few times, then stretched out his legs and his pant leg shifted, revealing just a glimpse of his prosthetic.

Across the way, a family were having some food when the father nudged the mother and inclined his head toward Jack. A fierce protectiveness coursed through her veins as Karla watched the man get up, looking to his wife before he crouched down in front of the little boy with them, and then, as they both moved, Karla saw that the maybe seven-year-old had a prosthetic too.

Jack sat up straighter as the man came closer, the child clinging to his father's leg. Karla watched as Jack glanced down at the boy's leg, then flashed him the biggest grin Karla had ever seen on him. He bent over and rolled up the leg of his pants, and Karla watched in amazement as the boy's eyes went wide, like he couldn't believe that Jack was like him.

Luke had woken up during all the commotion, and then both Jack and Luke had invited the child to hang out with them. When Luke and Jack had tired him out and he had fallen asleep, the boy's father had thanked Luke, but especially Jack, having explained that his son had lost his leg from sepsis and had been very withdrawn.

Karla listened as she heard Jack say to the father that it was hard for him too, losing his leg and that it had taken him a long time to come to terms with it. Jack even gave the father his number and said to call him anytime, and he would love to have his new friend at Rebel Racers sometime in the future.

It had been a different side to Jack that did nothing to stop Karla from being attracted to him.

When they had arrived in the UK, Jack drove them to their hotel, then told Luke he was not sitting in his room all night and they were all going for food and maybe a pint. There was a steakhouse across the road from the hotel, so once they were showered and rested, all three of them had gone to the steakhouse, and Karla enjoyed finding out a little bit more about Jack and Luke, their childhood, and sharing some stories about the things Emil and Oskar got up to as children and teens.

When Luke ducked back to the hotel to call Emil, Karla had expected Jack to not want to be alone with her, but he just waved off Luke's offer of cash and said that Luke could get dinner tomorrow night after the practice.

She and Jack had shared another drink and when she yawned, Jack had teased her that his company must be boring as fuck if she was fit to fall asleep. Karla had teased him back, saying she had not slept on the boat like the two men had and hadn't napped before dinner. Jack had laughed, calling for the bill, then rolled his eyes when Karla tried to pay.

They had walked back to the hotel in silence, stopping at their respective bedroom doors and Jack had given her this little lopsided smile as he said goodnight, waiting till she had gone inside before going inside himself.

Today, after breakfast, they had gone out to the forest and Karla really hadn't much to do besides making sure that all the equipment that Luke and Jack needed had arrived and that the two navigators NLQ Racing had hired for the two days had turned up. Once all her checks were done, she stood to the side, and watched Jack walk around his rally car, checking the tires, and doing other things that Karla had no clue about.

It was super muddy in this staging area and she was glad that Luke had talked her into wearing appropriate footwear so she wasn't up to her knees in muck. Luke had already finished putting on his race suit and getting in his car to put on his helmet, but Jack, who had also pulled on his race suit, was sat in his car, his jaw set.

It was then Karla realized that Jack needed to take off his prosthetic leg to slot into the custom one in the car, but the ground was too muddy for him to hop somewhere he could put his everyday leg safely. And the stubborn man was not going to ask for help.

Karla strode over to the car and crouched down, resting her hands on Jack's knees without thinking. "I'll take your prosthetic."

Jack looked like he was about to argue, then sighed. "I supposed at least this time, I'm not chucking it at ya and you nearly dropping it."

"And you aren't calling me a stripper. At least we have made some progress."

Jack barked out a laugh that made his eyes twinkle with mischief as he undid his attachments and handed Karla his prosthetic. She took hold of it, carefully and was about to turn around when she heard Jack say. "Thanks, Karla."

Karla nodded, then headed over to Jack's ordinary car, and put the prosthetic in the back seat of the car, where it would be safe. Then she hoisted herself onto a bench that had been fashioned from wood and watched Jack and Luke take off.

It seemed like hours before they stopped for lunch, and then took off again. She was glad that the weather stayed dry, and relatively cool so that the two men could enjoy the practice and just have fun. Sometime in the early afternoon, the two men pulled up alongside one another and Karla walked over to stand between the two cars and ask if they needed anything.

Jack and Luke talked in terms that Karla was starting to get to understand after spending time with the two men and doing her own studying. Jack's navigator got out of the car and fist-bumped with Jack. Luke got out to stretch his legs, rotating his hips and Karla asked him if he was okay.

"I'm grand, Karla. Just gonna take a bit to get used to the intensity of driving again. The sim is great practice but the real thing is the test I need. I thought I'd feel worse but it'll be grand."

Luke walked off, and Karla leaned in the passenger side and looked at Jack. "You good?"

Jack grinned like an idiot. "Hell ya! There was a sketchy moment there when the back kicked out and I swear the backend nearly kissed a tree but fucking hell it was brill."

Karla narrowed her gaze, utterly confused. "I don't understand much of what you said. What is a sketchy moment?"

He looked at her for a moment, as if checking to see if she was serious, then laughed. "It means, um, shady or like dangerous. So like hitting the tree would have been dangerous. I'm not explaining it right...fuck...I can show ya though...hop in."

Now it was Karla's turn to look at him. "You want me to go in the car?"

Jack shrugged. "I mean, if I'm stuck with ya, ya might as well know what it's like to be in a rally car. I know the route now, so you don't need to shout directions at me or anything...come on, I bet you'll enjoy it."

Karla was about to say no. She was about to decline Jack's offer because it sounded like madness for her to accept his offer and be a passenger in a rally car. This was the kind of thing that Oskar and Emil would do. They were the adrenaline junkies, not Karla.

But hadn't coming to Ireland been a leap of faith? Hadn't she taken a risk by moving countries and starting over? Could she put her trust in Jack to keep her safe in the forest?

He was looking at her expectantly, his grin slowly fading as if Karla's rejection would undo all the progress they'd made. Karla let her lips curve into a smile as she heard herself say. "I need a helmet, right?"

CHAPTER SEVENTEEN

Jack

THAT SMILE.

That goddamn sexy smile that was twisting Jack's insides up in a way he had never felt before. There had been moments over the last couple days, times when Jack caught Karla watching him, or when her features softened and she gave him that smile that made him long to feel that smile against his lips.

It wasn't a good idea, this crush or attraction he had to Karla. And it certainly wasn't the best idea to have her in the car beside him, with nowhere to go. Her smell, that citrussy scent of her shampoo would linger in the car, on he would lay awake the entire night remembering how fucking fantastic Karla had smelled.

Right now, the navigator that had been loaned to Jack for the two days was fastening a helmet onto Karla. She didn't need a race suit because he wasn't gonna go full speed, just go fast enough to give Karla a glimpse of why Jack loved it.

After the accident, Jack never thought he'd want to get in

a car again and drive on the limit, and it had taken a fuckton of therapy for Jack to realize that he wasn't his Da, and he could still love everything about being in motorsport even if a car was what took his leg.

The door opened and Karla climbed in and turned toward him. "Okay, I'm ready to go."

Jack heard the excitement in her tone, the eagerness, and damn him to hell but he wanted to hear that excitement in her voice and her be naked in his bed. He relaxed he had been staring at her for a heartbeat too long when Karla started to frown.

"Have you changed your mind?"

Jack shook his head, trying to shove his lustful thoughts to the back of his mind. "Nah, just wondering if you get car sick or motion sickness or whatever?"

"Nope. I used to sled down the steep slope in our village when we were children. And I've driven ATV's before. You don't need to worry."

Karla took the shoulder belts in her hands and then frowned. Jack watched her for a minute, then realized he was gonna have to do up the seatbelt for her. That meant he had to touch her. Get closer.

Trying not to let himself think too hard, Jack took a deep breath. "Let me. We need to make sure that you are locked and loaded or Emil will kill me by proxy." Karla narrowed her gaze like she didn't understand, so Jack continued. "If you come back with so much as a papercut, Luke will take it upon himself to make me bleed, because your big brother isn't here, but his man is."

Karla laughed, a deep throaty sound that sent blood rushing to a part of Jack's anatomy that he should not be even contemplating using for the same reason as him making sure that Karla was strapped in tight.

Emil and Luke would fucking gut him.

Jack clicked the seatbelt in place and tugged to make sure they were secure. "I know you said you got this, but if it gets too much, don't try and act the tough guy and ride it out. I'm not being a nag, okay? This is about your safety and your well-being. I won't fuck about with that."

Karla blinked, like she was surprised that he would even care. That made his stomach twist in a knot because he knew that he was the reason why she had given him that look. He'd been an absolute prick to her since the day they'd met and that was something that Jack couldn't take back.

Before Jack could utter an apology, a sharp rap of knuckles on the window on Karla's side made him jerk back as Luke's face loomed and he motioned for Karla to put down the window. She looked at him, and he just shrugged, then proceeded to lower the window.

"Um, nope. Not happening. Emil would kill me."

Jack was about to tell Luke that Karla was perfectly safe, and bit back a grin as Karla glared at Luke. "My brother is not my keeper, Luke, and neither are you. How can I truly stand and answer queries if I do not understand why it is that you and Jack do what you do?"

"It's not like going on a roller coaster, Karla."

Karla shook her head. "I left Denmark because I wanted to live my life and not the life my mother had planned for me. I wanted to be free to take chances, to experience everything I possibly could instead of living day in, day out, under constant supervision. This is my choice and I want to do this. You cannot stop me."

There was a backbone of steel in this woman. Her words were determined, her intentions clear. He hadn't known that one of the reasons Karla had come to Ireland was because her mother had been stifling her, had been trying to hold her back and be something that she didn't want to be.

Karla would never be like his Ma. She would never stand by as her husband drank away the money you'd earned and had to beg from neighbours for food. How his Ma would cower in corners when his Da came in stinking of whiskey and smoke, shouting the odds when food wouldn't magically appear on the table, with him having spent the money and all.

"Luke, I'm not gonna go full tilt. I swear down. I'm the last person who wants to cause an accident and see Karla get hurt. I'm gonna take her down the lake pass, give her a taste but nothing too reckless."

Luke looked from Jack to Karla, then back at Jack. "You'll behave?"

Jack held up three fingers. "Scouts honour."

Luke snorted. "Like fuck you were in the scouts."

"Nah, got kicked out after a week," Jack said with a shrug. "But the sentiment is still there. C'mon, Luke, this is the last chance we get to do this for just fun, and who knows when we will be able to let Karla have this chance again."

Luke relented, and Jack gave Karla a second to change her mind before he put his foot to the floor and took off. This was when Jack felt the most free. The most alive and it was obvious from the little squeals and excited laughter that Karla was feeling it too. Jack didn't dare look at her, because if he did, if he saw the look of exhilaration on her face, it would end him.

As he came down the slope, leading to the little verge by the lake, Jack did a move called a Scandinavian Flick, where he turned the car slightly in the opposite direction that he intended to turn, and yanked the steering wheel back in the direction he wanted to turn, to drift around the corner and then he stopped the car on the embankment by the lake.

Jack let the car idle, and shifted slightly in the car so that he could look at Karla. Her cheeks were flushed, her lips were slightly parted and she had this excited look in her eyes as she turned to Jack, and they both took off their helmets, resting them in their laps.

"Oh my god, that was amazing. I mean you were going so fast and you were doing all these turns and when you went over the ridge it felt like we were flying! Flying, Jack! And my stomach was tumbling and adrenaline, I've never felt like that before and I can see why you and Luke do this, and I'm rambling, I don't ram-"

Jack's control snapped, and before he knew it, he was unlocking his seatbelt with one hand on her own seatbelt, Jack sort of pulled her toward him, and crashed his lips against hers. Her lips were warm, soft and he moaned low in his throat as she sucked in a breath, parting her lips, and then Jack deepened the kiss by sweeping his tongue into her mouth.

His heart was racing, his blood on fire as Karla, seemingly over her shock kissed him back, her hand landing on his knee as if to steady herself and Jack wished they weren't in a car, and he could kiss her properly, and quench this need that he had for her.

The roar of an engine sounded not too far away and they broke apart, staring at one another with wide eyes. Karla looked shocked, her lips kiss swollen and Jack wanted to kiss her all over again. He leaned toward her, and she toward him, but Luke's rally car came into view. Luke stopped his car on Karla's side of the car, rolled down his window and Karla did the same.

"Well, how was it?"

Karla glanced over at Jack, her cheeks pinking, before she snapped her gaze back to Luke. "It's...it's....I don't think I've processed it all yet. But I can certainly see why you guys do this."

Luke grinned. "I know, right? C'mon, let's head back. I'm starving."

He took off then, and Karla slowly put on her helmet, fastened it, and proceeded to stare out the window, looking at everything but Jack. The drive back was torture in a way Jack had never comprehended before.

Chapter Eighteen

Karla

KARLA HAD NOT BEEN EXPECTING Jack to kiss her.

She certainly had not expected to kiss him back.

Karla couldn't stop thinking about the kiss and what might have happened if they had not been interrupted by Luke. She had not been able to make sense of it all in her head and she could almost taste the disappointment from Jack when she had put back on her helmet, then looked out the window.

When Jack had brought the car to a halt back at the main site, she had turned to say something to Jack, but he had unhooked himself from his driving leg, and whistled for one of the navigators to grab his leg, glancing only at Karla to find out where she had placed his everyday prosthetic.

Her mind had been still on the kiss as they locked things up for the night, and even more so when Luke asked what they were doing for dinner and Jack had yawned, telling them he was gonna crash and order room service. Luke had looked at Karla, like Jack's idea was very tempting but he hadn't wanted to leave her alone.

Karla had hugged Luke, telling him that she was tired too and they needed to rest so they were fully rested for the football game the next day. Jack had been closing his door when she had come to open hers, and Karla opened her mouth to say something but Jack had closed the door with a firm click.

After a fitful night's sleep, Karla had woken early, showered, and dressed in jeans and Emil's team shirt with his number and Anderson on the back. When Emil had found out that they were going to the match in Manchester, he had sent Karla a jersey, telling her she had to wear it. Luke had one too, so when Karla walked down into the reception area to meet Luke for breakfast.

He grinned when he saw Karla in the jersey, then said. "We're just waiting for sleeping beauty to arrive and then we could grab some breakfast to go? It's not that long of a trip to Manchester but traffic might be a bitch."

Karla nodded, then glanced behind her when Luke swore. Jack swagged down the corridor, dressed in jeans, a backwards baseball cap, and a Manchester United jersey. When he saw the look on Luke's face, Jack just shrugged. "Don't gimmie that look."

"Why the hell are you wearing that?"

Jack stood next to Karla, a slight smile curving his lips. It made her think of kissing him again. And that made her feel a little insane.

"I'm a United fan. Born and bred. My Da would..."

Jack's voice trailed off and Karla wanted to reach out and touch him, however, Jack just shook his head and walked out the door, leaving Luke and Karla to follow after him. They stopped in the car and grabbed food to go, then Luke and Karla chatted in the car while Jack just ate his food and looked out the window.

When they arrived at Old Trafford, Karla stood to the side while Jack and Luke signed autographs, with Jack laughing when some of the away team supporters booed him. Luke played up on it too, messing about and then they were being escorted to the box, and handed drinks as refreshments.

They chatted to some of the other famous people, and then Jack walked over to the side and drank his beer, looking out at the pitch as the players came out to warm up. Luke was chatting to some man who worked with an Irish security firm, and Karla wandered over to where Jack stood. She leaned on the rail beside him, though waited for him to take the lead, and after a few minutes, he finally did.

"I always wanted to come here, yano." He said quietly, taking another sip of beer before he continued. "and we had planned to go for me birthday. I saved all my confirmation money and me Da found it, then went out on a bender."

"A bender?" Karla asked, a little confused.

Jack sighed, letting out a snort. "Went out and got blind ass drunk. Spent all the money I'd saved up. He'd fucking be pissed as hell to see me here now in a fancy box and all this free drink."

Karla nudged him with her shoulder. "I was raised not to speak ill of the dead, but your father sounded like a røvhul."

Jack barked out a laugh. "Ya, he fucking was."

They looked at each other, and that spark, that draw that had been there in the car came roaring back, but then Jack blinked and glanced to where Luke had come up to stand with them as the match was about to kick off.

Luke cheered and whooped when Emil came onto the pitch, making Karla laugh when he commented how sexy Emil looked. Jack kept his eyes focused on the start of the game, and Karla pushed thoughts of kisses and drunks out of her mind to watch her big brother play the game he loved.

Karla remembered the first time she had seen Emil playing

football professionally, how the entire family had watched with pride as he had stood and sang the national anthem even though he had a voice that would crack glass. The memory made Karla smile as she pulled herself out of her head to focus on the game.

She cheered and shouted when Emil got the ball, when he passed to one of his teammates, and they swore when someone tackled him. It was an exciting game, action non-stop and Karla was loving all of it. She would have to make sure to take the time to come watch Emil play more often.

Karla blinked, and then, she scanned the pitch for her brother. Everything happened in slow motion, like a dream, so much so that Karla wondered if she was imagining it. Her eyes were on Emil as he just suddenly crumpled to the ground and did not get back up. The referee blew his whistle, as one of Emil's teammates dropped to his knees, shook Emil, and then he was gesturing wildly.

"Why isn't he getting up? Come on, babe, stop messing about." Luke mumbled, concern on his face.

Her heart was pounding so much she could hear it, as she leaned forward and then watched as the other football player started to do chest compressions on Emil. She heard Luke mutter something like, *"Don't do this to me, you can't leave me"* as medics rushed onto the pitch.

Players were visibly upset, crying openly as their respective managers tried to usher them down the tunnel, but they refused to leave the pitch. Karla couldn't see Emil now for the crowd blocking him from view and she needed to see him.

As if the Gods heard her, the crowd parted. Emil had been lifted onto a stretcher, his shirt ripped apart and he was being shocked, her brave, beautiful brother's body jerking as the medics crossed the pitch and Karla knew that her brother was going to die.

The man who had loved and protected Karla her entire life

was going to die.

And she couldn't remember if she told him she loved him when they last spoke.

Karla heard someone's choked sob and only realised it was coming from her when strong arms came around her, turning her from the chaos going on and pulling her into his chest.

"Hey, don't look. Just close your eyes. I've got you. He'll be grand. It's okay."

Jack kissed the top of her head and that act of kindness undid her, Karla's knees buckled, but Jack held her up, holding her to him. A throat cleared and Karla stepped out of Jack's embrace but slipped her hand into his. The security man that Luke had been talking to had come over, gripping Luke on the shoulder, and giving him a solemn look.

"They are taking Emil to the hospital. It looks like he might have had a heart attack. He's alive. I wish I had more news. Your car is waiting downstairs to bring you to him. I'll lead ya down."

Luke stood there, unable to move, and Karla had to let go of Jack's hand to go to him. She wrapped her arms around him and squeezed him hard. He hugged her back, and she could feel his tears against her skin.

"He has only just found the love of his life. He will not stop fighting to come back to you."

Luke seemed to believe her, because he started to walk toward the door. Karla glanced over her shoulder and Jack was there, slipping his hand into her. He shielded her from the whispers and the pointed looks, until they were in the car and then he hugged her to him.

Emil was the heart that kept their family together. If he died, if they lost him, Karla would lose a piece of herself and she was not sure that she could go on without him. Luke was crying softly next to Karla and she rested a hand on his knee, trying to offer him a little comfort.

CHAPTER NINETEEN

Jack

JACK FUCKING HATED HOSPITALS.

He hated the smell of antiseptic, the white walls that seemed to be a prerequisite for all goddamn hospitals, the constant beep of machines, and the general overwhelming sense of doom that seemed to seep into your marrow the moment you stepped over the threshold.

He tried to sit up in the bed, felt a little off balance, and then his eyes landed on his legs...

"Your leg was crushed in the collision, Jack. You were bleeding out and they were left with no option but to remove the limb to free you from the vehicle."

Jack couldn't stop looking at his legs.

"You put it back on, right? Like they do on the telly?" He hated the pleading in his tone.

The doctor gave a shake of her head. "I'm very sorry, Jack. There was no saving your leg."

Jack ripped the blankets off his body and looked down to where his right leg came to a halt just above the knee. He stared at it, the space where his leg used to be, and then suddenly, someone was screaming and screaming.

It took Jack a few minutes to realize that the person screaming was him.

Jack's leg bounced as he tried to push down the memories of waking up and finding out that he'd lost his leg, his Da, and his baby sister. They haunted him, those memories, even now when he had accepted the loss of his limb, and all the crap that came with it.

He was trying to reign in his disdain for hospitals and focus on the woman who was clung to his side, her hand still in his. She had yet to let go of his hand since she'd grasped it back at the football stadium. Jack could almost feel the worry coming off her skin, and that was even before you took in the man wearing a hole in the floor.

Luke hadn't stopped pacing since they had been ushered into this room, with a promise to give them an update on Emil's condition once they had news. Luke and Karla had been avoiding phone calls, though Karla had taken a call from her sister, speaking in Danish and crying a little.

Luke's phone rang and he yanked it out of his pocket, looked at the screen, then lifted his gaze to Karla. "It's Oskar."

"Answer it. He will keep ringing until one of us does."

Luke inclined his head, then pressed answer on the phone before putting it on speaker. "Oskar, I have you on speaker."

"What news have you?"

Jack had only met Oskar a handful of times but knew that the Danish man wasn't one for small talk, and he was direct in his words and actions. He had liked that about Oskar and knew it must be killing him to be so far away from the man who was like a brother to him.

"There's been no news yet. We're still waiting."

A sigh sounded down the phone. "Karla?"

"I'm here, Oskar."

There was a moment of silence and Karla squeezed Jack's hand before they heard Oskar speak once again. "Your brother is strong. He is stubborn. Too stubborn to let whatever had him collapsing to get the better of him. You hear me?"

"I do." Karla croaked out and Jack leaned closer into her, for support.

"Luke?" Oskar said down the phone.

"Ya?"

"He would not leave you when he has just found you. Emil would defy the gods to be with you. He loves you. Stay strong for him. I'm awaiting confirmation of the next flight home. I will be there as soon as I can."

Luke sat down on the seat behind him, the first time that he had rested since they arrived. "Emil would give out to ya for making a fuss. He would tell you that Quinn needs you now, not him."

"Quinn was the one who rang the airline to arrange a ticket."

The door to the waiting room opened and a doctor stepped in, and it felt like the entire room just froze. The doctor looked at the phone in Luke's hand, then gave them a tight smile.

"I'm Doctor Field, Emil's doctor."

Karla jerked to her feet, her hand still in Jack's. "Please, is my brother alive?"

The doctor nodded, and Karla sat down, a sob escaping her lips, and Jack slipped his hand from Karla's and wrapped his arms around her.

"Emil suffered a sudden cardiac event, but he is awake and talking. We need to do further testing to establish exactly what caused the cardiac event, but he is receiving the best possible care."

"Can we see him?" Luke asked, clutching the phone tightly in his hand.

"Not all of you, but maybe just one. He needs to get some rest and we still have lots of tests to run to make sure that this does not happen again."

Luke slumped in his car, and lifted his gaze to Karla's, opening his mouth to speak but Karla cut across him.

"You go to him, Luke."

"Karla, you're his sister. You should go."

Karla smiled at Luke. "And you are the love of his life. Kiss him once for you and then once for me. He would much rather see your handsome face than my tear-stained one."

"She's right, Luke. Emil will want to see you." Oskar said down the phone. "Quinn got me a flight in a couple of hours, so tell Emil I will kick his ass for making us all fret so much. Drama queen."

Then Oskar hung up the phone, and Luke went with the doctor to see Emil, leaving Jack and Karla alone. His arms were still around her, and Karla didn't seem like she was gonna let go of him any time soon. So Jack just held her, and tried to be there for her in any way he could.

"I remember when I was younger," Karla began, her hand landing on his chest and he was terrified that she would feel how fast his heart was beating. "It wasn't long after Dad's accident, and the money had dried up because we had to pay for medical bills. Emil was in trouble for skipping school to work on the fishing boat, and our mother was falling apart."

Jack ran his hand up and down Karla's arms, comforting her as she continued to speak. "There was this group of girls who were wealthier than us, their parents had houses while we had cabins. They called me fish girl and made fun of my dad. Then Emil came back to school and told them all that he would hurt their brothers if they continued to hurt me."

Jack smiled, and ran a hand over Karla's hair. "He was being your brother."

"He has always, always tried to protect me. And when he

fell, there was no one to protect him. There must have been signs that he was unwell. Why didn't I see it?"

"You heard the doc, Karla. Sudden cardiac event. I'm not a doctor or anything but I think the name implied that there were no signs. I've seen it happen before. And those athletes were grand. Emil will be grand."

Karla shifted to look up at him, her eyes wide and then she was arching toward him and Jack felt like a shitty human being because he wanted to kiss her so bad, but her brother almost died, and kissing her would be taking advantage, right?

Jack was saved from having to make that decision by the door opening and Karla jumped out of his arms to stand. Luke stood in the doorway, looking from Karla to Jack, before he looked back at Karla.

"Emil is threatening to get out of bed or to sign himself out if you don't go see him. He argued with the doctor so much that his heartrate increased so they said you can come back and see him too."

Jack looked at Karla as she let loose a laugh. "That sounds like something Emil would do."

He made to get up, then felt a sharp pain in his knee had him exhaling sharply. For a moment, Jack felt like he wanted to throw up, and Jack wasn't sure if he took a step forward would he be able to retain his balance.

"Jack? Are you okay?"

Plastering a smile on his face, Jack nodded his head. "I'm grand. Leg's just stiff from sitting down. Go see your brother."

Both Karla and Luke starred at him, but he could visibly see the worry in Karla's eyes. Jack ran a hand through his hair, then took a step forward, ignored the pang of pain. "I'm gonna take a walk and loosen out my muscles. I'll be fine. Go see Emil."

Karla gave him a small smile, then followed Luke out of the room and Jack almost collapsed into the car, stifled a groan because his leg was throbbing so much that he felt dizzy. He'd kept putting it off, getting his stump looked at and Jack could feel the wrongness down there. Jack lied to himself that it wasn't that bad. That he just needed some antibiotic cream and he would be grand.

CHAPTER TWENTY

Karla

KARLA WAS EXHAUSTED. She hadn't slept since the night before Emil's accident, and both herself and Luke had remained at the hospital until the doctor told them they needed to leave so Emil could get some rest. They had all gone back to the hotel, and Karla had spent the night with Luke in his room as they tried to make arrangements.

In the end, it was Jack who suggested that they stay here with Luke, and he would travel back with the cars, and that he'd already spoken to Shane, who would get them on a flight when they needed it. Karla had been grateful to Jack for being there, for his support and she wanted to thank him, but when she woke this morning, and headed to his room, Jack had already checked out.

After making Luke shower and eat, they had gone back to the hospital to check on Emil. As they were about to head into Emil's room, Karla's phone rang and she closed her eyes when she saw it was her mother on the other end of the phone.

"You want me to talk to her?" Luke offered, his eyes moving to the door.

Karla put her hand on his arm. "Go and make sure my brother isn't up to devilment. I'll deal with your future mother-in-law."

Luke flushed a vivid shade of red that had Karla laughing, before she answered her phone.

"Hey Mom."

"Karla, I want to speak to Emil. I have called and called him, and he will not answer."

Karla rolled her eyes. "Mom, like I explained yesterday, Emil is resting, and Luke has his phone. We were just about to head in to get an update on Emil. I will call you with an update later."

Her mother shifted down the line. "I told Laerke that she needed to book me a flight to go see my son, but she said that there would be enough time for that later. You know I don't know anything about that internet thing. You need to speak to your sister and tell her I need her to book me a flight."

The phone was plucked from Karla's hand and Karla whirled round to see a very haggard Oskar standing holding her phone. He gave her a small smile, then spoke into the phone.

"Karla is correct. It would only stress him out if he thought his beloved mother had made that long trip when he is perfectly fine. You have my word that I will ensure that you are told if that changes."

Oskar nodded at something her mother said to him, and then he spoke again. "You need to stay to make sure that Laerke looks after herself and your grandchild. Let me make sure that Emil, Karla, and Luke are looking after themselves."

After a few more minutes, Oskar hung up and handed Karla her phone, then held open his arms. She went to him, knowing that there wasn't many people that Oskar offered open affection to. For the longest time, Karla had been a little bit in love with Oskar, but he had never treated her as anything but Emil's little sister.

She stepped back from his embrace, and looked at him, really looked at him. There was nothing left of the spark of attraction she had once felt for Oskar, her mind drifting back to the blistering kiss in a rally car and a man who excited and infuriated her.

"I did not think that you would come, and not so quickly."

Oskar rubbed his knuckles against her chin. "I saw him fall on a TV screen and I was frozen. It was Quinn who held me up when I saw them doing CPR. If it was terrifying for me to see it happen, then it must have been even more so for you to see it happening right in front of you."

"It matters not now. Emil is alive and that is all that matters."

Oskar offered her another smile, and that made Karla look at him again. When she stared at him a little too long, Oskar arched a brow, making Karla laugh.

"I am trying to figure out what happened to that boy who didn't know how to smile. I think your Quinn is a good influence on you, Oskar."

"She is the best thing to ever happen to ever happen to me, Karla. Besides Emil that is."

Karla grinned, touching Oskar gently on the arm. "I think, romantic that he is, that Emil would tell you that you do not need to include him in that sentiment. I am glad that you are happy, Oskar."

They started to head toward Emil's hospital room, when Oskar asked her if she had any interest in any Irish boys yet. Karla's steps faltered and she might have fallen, had Oskar not grabbed her.

"There is an Irish boy...does Emil know?"

"It's...no...I mean..." Karla stopped dead and looked at Oskar. "No, Emil does not know because there is nothing to tell. We kissed. That's all. And he doesn't like me...I don't even like him. He is stubborn and infuriating and argumentative and reckless."

Oskar's face was expressionless for a moment and then he burst out laughing, startling Karla. When he managed to stop laughing and took in Karla's unamused expression, Oskar grinned. "That was what I thought about Quinn when we first met. She got under my skin, with her attitude and stubbornness. She wouldn't let me look after her, and it infuriated me. And now look at us."

Karla opened her mouth, then closed it, then opened it again.

"Do not say a word to Emil, Oskar. He will fret and it will not aid his recovery."

Oskar's gaze narrowed. "Do we know who he is? Do I need to have a word with him about his intentions?"

Karla chuckled, mock-slapping him before she walked into Emil's hospital room. Her brother was sitting up in bed, hooked up to all kinds of wires. He and Luke were holding hands, and then Emil turned to give her a small smile.

"Karla, come in and make Luke stop fussing. I told him that I am fine, but the foolish man won't listen to me."

"Perhaps, if you were less of an attention seeker, then your boyfriend would not fuss over you." Oskar said as he came to stand in the doorway, and Karla watched as Emil's face broke out into a smile.

"Oska," Emil sighed, using the moniker Emil had given him when they were children. "You should not have come all this way to see me. Your Quinn needs you."

Oskar went over and put his hand on Emil's forehead. "My Quinn wanted to come with me to make sure that you and Luke were okay, but she knew that with you both being athletes that you would scold her if she came too. She said, and I paraphrase, stop playing the martyr and get your ass out of bed."

Emil laughed, and then the laugh turned into a sob as Emil started to cry in earnest, startling everyone in the room. Oskar sat on the bed, and pulled Emil to him, patting his back. Luke lifted his gaze to Karla, and swallowed hard, before he started to talk with emotion thick in his voice.

"The doctor said that Emil has an issue with his heart. He had a cardiac arrest. The doctor said this happened because the electrical impulses that regulate heartbeats don't function properly. They want him to get fitted with an Implantable Cardioverter Defibrillator."

Karla sat down on the chair beside the bed, and rested her hand on Emil's leg.

"They said that he could return to playing over time. But it was a wait-and-see kind of thing."

Oskar leaned back, and gripped Emil by the shoulders. "You will have the operation, and you will do what the doctors say. You will take your time and doing that, doing all that they tell you will ensure that you are back playing the game you love before too long. This is not the end; this is a setback."

"A setback. It is just a setback." Emil said, and her brother nodded, taking a deep breath and he let Luke swipe away tears. "Okay. Okay."

"Good," said Oskar, a smile curving his lips. "So you will have the operation, and stop being a drama queen. It is not all about you, you know."

Emil chuckled, shaking his head, his lip trembling like he might cry again. "You should not have come all this way, Oskar, but I am glad you did. Thank you for being here. All of you. Thank you."

Luke got up and kissed Emil on the cheek, and Karla gave his leg another squeeze while Oskar gave Emil's shoulders one final squeeze, and they stayed there, mostly talking about idle things, and not about the operation Emil would need in the next few days.

This was what being family was all about, showing up and just being there when they were needed, and Karla knew that they would do so for as long as Emil needed them. Today, Karla thanked the gods that her brother was alive, and everything else would find its way to being all right.

CHAPTER TWENTY-ONE

Jack

JACK HAD BEEN HOME for about a week now, and he knew he was in trouble. Once he had walked in the door to his apartment, and removed his prosthetic, the infection and swelling was so bad that he hadn't been able to put his leg back on. Jack had sent Shane an email to say he had a virus and would be out of the gym and that for a few days.

When he had realized his infection was slightly worse than just something that would go away if he ignored it. He used some antibiotic cream, hoping that would do the trick, but his stump still was angry and swollen.

So Jack gave in and called his GP, looking to get her to come see him at his apartment, because he couldn't get his prosthetic on to drive, and he'd been a stubborn bastard when he'd purchased his car, and stayed away from an automatic. The conversation hadn't gone well.

"Can I help you?" Said the voice on the end of the line.

"I need to arrange for the doc to come visit me. My name's Jack O'Neill."

There was a dramatic pause and chewing gum pop. "We don't do house calls."

Jack sighed, shifting on the couch. "Dr. Molloy knows my situation and will call out to me."

"Dr. Molloy is on maternity leave and the temp doesn't do house calls. You'll have to come to the surgery yourself. I can give you an appointment for the 15th at like four."

Jack was starting to lose patience and it didn't help that his stump was throbbing.

"Listen, sweetheart, I can't come to the bloody surgery, hence why I asked for a goddamn home visit. If you just let me speak to the temp doctor, I can explain."

"I'm sorry, Mr. O'Neill, but the doctor only speaks to patients who come to the surgery. Those are the rules. I'm sure that you can manage to get yourself to the surgery if you really need to see a doctor."

Jesus, fucking, Christ...He was gonna have to spell it out for her, wasn't he.

Through gritted teeth, Jack tried to be polite but he was quickly about to lose his shit. "As I said, I can't come to the surgery. If you look at my file you will see that I am an amputee, and I can't get my prosthetic back on."

"Like okay, but can you not just come in your wheelchair?"

"No," Jack ground out. "I don't have a wheelchair and haven't needed one since I left the hospital with my prostheses. And can I just say how fucking rude it is that you are, sounding so bloody ableist."

The woman clucked. She fucking clucked at him.

"Right, since this is going fucking fabulous, if you can't get me a house call, then can you get the doctor to send a prescription to my local pharmacy and they'll deliver the antibiotics. Tell the doctor I have an infection in my stump due to a prosthetic that didn't quite fit."

"The doctor won't write you a script unless you present your-

*self for examination at the surgery. So I have that appointment
on the fifteenth if you want it."*

Jack snapped, his temper frayed. *"Are you for fucking real? I.
Can't. Come. To. The. Surgery. Get that through your thick
fucking skull. I need a doctor to come see me and if you can't
arrange that or a goddamn prescription, then if the infection
gets any worse and they end up chipping off what's left of me leg,
I'll fucking drag myself to the surgery, and beat ya with the cut
off fucking piece of flesh ya fecking eejit!"*

Of course, the receptionist had hung up on him...

Jack had flung his phone away in frustration. After
growling and wishing he could punch something or someone,
Jack had gotten up and sort of clambered in the general direction of where he had thrown the phone.

Jack had been exhausted then, and he'd just sat down on
the floor, resting his head against the wall. He had texted Luke
to see how Emil was, hell, he'd even texted Karla to check-in.

That kiss.

That fucking kiss that upended his world and tilted it on
its axis.

It replied over and over in his mind, with Jack unable to
make sense of it all. Yes, Karla was fucking beautiful. Yes, Jack
wanted her like he had never wanted anyone else as much as he
wanted Karla, but how the hell were the two of them
supposed to be a thing?

That wasn't something that Jack could even think about
then. When he had summoned the strength to get up, considering that there was no way that he was getting a doctor's
appointment, now, Jack went and raided his medicine cabinet.
He had all his daily meds on the counter, so he rarely went in
there, and he emptied it out.

He felt like he had struck gold when he found a handful of
antibiotics left over from his last prescription. He'd been
prescribed them for like ten days, and ended up only taking

them for like five days, stopping when he had felt better. Jack also found some steroids he'd never bothered to take and since he wasn't convinced that these meds ever went off, Jack just said to hell with it and took um, determined to see how he got on.

Today, Jack had gotten up and taken a shower, the water piercing his skin. He'd felt so weak that he'd had to use the shower seat because he wasn't entirely sure that he could hold himself up. After showering and getting dressed in joggers and a tee, Jack also pulled on a hoody, because despite the sweat on his forehead, he was fucking freezing.

His stomach was a little queasy, so Jack forced himself to eat some toast, and wash it down with a cup of tea. His phone rang, but he sent his Ma to voicemail and made sure to take the last of his meds. They weren't doing much for his infection. Neither was the cream and he was nearly out. Jack had read somewhere that some antibiotics and steroids didn't kick in until a couple of days after you started taking them.

So, he should start to see an improvement in a few days right? There was nothing really to be worrying about or stressing about. He'd be grand. He'd be fine.

Jack got up off the kitchen stool, spots dancing in his eyes. His body trembled. Putting out his hand to the wall to steady himself. Christ, why was the room spinning? Why did his fucking couch look so far away?

"Da, pull over and let me fucking drive. You're gonna get us all killed."

Jack knew he was hallucinating, watching the scene unfold, just like the accident happened yesterday.

His Ma's crying made his ears ring.

"Shut up, Jack or I will throw ya out of this goddamn car while it's moving!"

His Da was standing in his front room now, drinking a

beer and smirking at him. Then his Da turned to him, and they were in the car once again.

His Da took his hand off the wheel, raising it as if to strike him, but it put the car off course and Jack reached out past his Da, grabbed the wheel, and gave it a yank.

The car headed straight toward the wall. His Ma was screaming. Jack had a moment to consider that he was about to die when the wall was suddenly there and the car went into it at speed.

Jack heard a scream of metal and then his world went black.

Then his Da was standing before him, face bloody, his grey t-shirt soaked with blood, and eyes that were dead looked at him.

"It was all your fault, Jack. You killed me. You killed your sister."

Jack shook his head. "That was you, Da, Not me. Not fucking me!"

His Da laughed at him, shaking his beer bottle at him. "Always playing the martyr aren't ya, Jack? Oh poor me, the cripple. My leg's gone and wah, wah, wah. Shut up and be a man, ya little shite."

Jack lunged for his da, filled with rage and guilt, forgetting for just that moment that he was missing a leg. He faceplanted to the floor, smacking his stump against the hardwood floor. Pain sliced through him, making him cry out, and then he rolled onto his back, staring at the ceiling as he tried to breathe through the pain.

He put his hand over his eyes, his chest heaving. Fuck. The infection was bad if he was sweating bullets and hallucinating his dead Da. He needed help. But who the hell could he call? There was no way he was calling his Ma, she'd freak out and be on his case. Jack would be grand in a bit. He just needed to rest his eyes for a minute and then he'd be okay.

Chapter Twenty-Two

Karla

Karla had arrived home yesterday after spending the week with Emil to help Luke as Emil recovered from his Implantable Cardioverter Defibrillator surgery. It had gone remarkably well, and Emil had been discharged to recover at home. She had left the couple to their own devices, on a promise that Luke would keep Karla up to date, and a warning that she would return if Emil did not behave.

She hadn't wanted to leave, however, Karla had also not wanted to take advantage of Andi and Shane's generosity, especially not when she had only just started her job. After she had showered and changed, Karla tried to call Jack to check in and got no answer.

Karla was worried that their kiss might have affected their working relationship and after a lot of thinking over the last few days, Karla had decided that she needed to be honest with Jack and tell him that nothing could happen between them.

Even if she really wanted it to.

That was how she found herself at his door that evening,

knocking twice on the door as she waited for an answer. She knew he should be home because his car was outside. When Jack didn't come to answer the door, she pulled out her phone, and dialed Jack's number. She could hear the phone ringing inside.

Karla knocked again. "Jack, it's Karla. Are you home?"

She was just about to leave when she heard a noise from inside. She knocked again and called his name, hoping he wasn't hurt or something. The horrid thought crossed her mind that Jack might right now have female company and it twisted something in her gut to think of him inside with another woman.

"Karla? The uh...the doors open. I just can't open it for ya."

That struck Karla as strange. She twisted the handle and pushed open the door, walking into the apartment. She spotted Jack right away. He was sitting up against the couch, sweating and looking rather pale.

"Jack, what happened to you?" Karla said as she dropped down to her knees and lifted her hand to his forehead. He was burning up even as he shivered.

Jack ducked his head. "I, uh, fuck. I got an infection and no doctor would do a house call and I couldn't put on my prosthetic. I got angry and threw my phone and couldn't call for someone to come get me."

Karla wasn't sure what to do so she did the only thing she could think of and called Shane, even though Jack protested. Shane told her that he was on his way home after dinner with Andi and a paramedic. Karla hung up and then went and got Jack some water, which he only sipped.

Setting the glass down on the table, Karla sank down to the floor beside him. "How long have you been here?"

Jack shrugged, a faint blush on his cheeks. "Couple of hours. I passed out for a bit but I'll be grand. I took some out-of-date antibiotics thinking they might help...guess they didn't."

Karla's gaze narrowed. "You cannot take out-of-date antibiotics, Jack. That is very dangerous."

Jack huffed out a breath and looked up at the ceiling. Karla was about to ask him a little more about his infection when the door opened. Anid, Shane, and a man Karla didn't know came in and Karla watched as Jack's jaw clenched.

Shane and Andi shared a concerned look while the man came right on over and Karla quickly moved out of his way. The man grinned at Jack, and then said. "Alright, Jack. My name's Connor and Andi's my future sister-in-law. I'm also a paramedic, so you mind if I give ya the once over?"

Karla watched as Jack's throat moved as he swallowed hard, then nodded. "My stump's infected. My driving prosthetic is a bit big so caused some friction. I should have sorted it sooner but I wanted in the car."

Connor opened his mouth to speak, but Karla cut across him "And why did you not say so and we could have done something?"

Karla had not meant to sound so harsh, and yet, she was a little bit furious with Jack for being so thick-skinned."

Andi came over and put her hand on Karla's shoulder, as Shane made a phone call. "It's cause he's a man! They don't like to ask for help and they would rather bulldoze through things rather than admit when something is up."

Connor snorted as he continued to examine Jack, rolled his eyes, and when Karla looked at Shane as he came back over, he gave a shrug. "Considering I was where Jack was not so long ago, I'm not going to argue with Andi."

As he sat back on his legs, Connor tilted his head at Jack. "Yup, that bad boy is infected. Looks very fucking angry, mate. Did you call your doctor?"

Jack snorted. "Ya, I did. The goddamn receptionist told

me that they don't do house calls at the moment, and in order to get a prescription, I'd have to see the doctor."

"Did you explain you couldn't get to the doctors?" Shane asked.

"Of course I did. Had to tell her I was a bloody amputee and couldn't get my prosthetic back on to drive. I was getting no sympathy from her, so ya, I got mad and flung me phone and have been sitting here ever since."

Connor reached out and rested his hand on Jack's shoulder. "I'm not a doctor, Jack, no matter how much Andi keeps dragging me in to do private consults like I'm Rebel PR's personal doc on call."

Andi grinned, and ruffled Connor's hair. "There must be some benefits to having to deal with you and the other two spanners. It's totally unfair that there are three of you."

Karla's mouth opened, then closed and Connor laughed. "Yup, identical triplets. And so not the point, Andrea."

"Before they start arguing," Shane interjected with a sigh, like it was something that he had to withstand quite often. "I made an appointment with the on-call doctor so we can drive you there and get ya sorted."

Jack glanced at the floor, his jaw clenched. Karla was worried he was going to refuse. Connor glanced over his shoulder and then back at Jack, who was trying to look anywhere but at them.

"Listen, me and Shane will give ya a hand. You have any crutches or anything you wanna use?"

"There's an old set in the closet in the hall." Jack mumbled through gritted teeth.

"I'll grab um." Andi said, walking back toward the front door.

Both Connor and Shane stood on either side of Jack, but he refused to look up at them. Karla didn't know what was going on, and she was about to say something when Shane and Connor exchanged a look, and then Shane gave her a smile.

"Why don't you run into Jack's room and grab him a hoodie? It's gone cold outside."

Karla opened her mouth to argue, but Andi, who had returned with the crutches and handed them off to Shane, nudged Karla's shoulder. "Come on, I'm sure we can both find something."

Still confused, Karla followed Andi, and then she heard Connor say to Jack. "She's gone now, mate. Let's get you up."

"Listen, Connor, I know we just met and all, but I'm bursting for a piss and I didn't want to fucking piss myself in front of her...not when I've already embarrassed meself enough."

Karla leaned against the wall, a sense of sadness washing over her. She hated that she was the reason Jack had been so uncomfortable. It must be so awful to be so strongly independent, and then to suddenly find you have to depend on others.

"Hey, it's not like it's the first time I've had to help a mate to the toilet. Only last week me and Shane here had to make sure a very drunk Hollywood heartthrob made it home safe and sound, and to his toilet, before he upchucked. His fiancée is not a woman I'd want to cross."

Andi came out with a hoodie, and handed it to Karla, with a soft smile on her face. "Men. They don't want to be vulnerable in front of the girl they like. And Jack, he's not used to letting anyone in."

Karla shook her head. "It's not like that. We've been professional."

Andi snorted. "I wasn't questioning that, Karla. But anyone with eyes can see the way he looks at you. If you're not interested, let him down gently mind. Behind that tough lad exterior, I think Jack's not used to having friends or people who care."

Jack came down the hall then, gave Karla a lopsided smile before he went into the bathroom, and closed the door behind him. She and Andi went back out to the living room, and the boys decided that they would take Jack to the doctors, and when they left, Karla decided she would stay, even after Andi went home, so that she could see how Jack was when he returned.

Chapter Twenty-Three

Jack

Having waved off Shane and Connor's offer to see him upstairs, and after agreeing to call Connor if he felt any worse, Jack made his way slowly upstairs. Connor had also been very insistent that Jack agree to come out for a drink with him, Shane, and Ronan Cusack, a bloody Hollywood star of all people, on their next boy's night.

Jack wasn't used to having guy friends. Hell, he wasn't used to having *any* friends. Luke was the closest thing to having a friend that Jack had in a long time and Jack had still tried to put up a wall, but something told Jack that Connor wasn't going to let him say no.

That had been confirmed when he had looked at Shane, who just shrugged, and told Jack that when Connor had helped him out with a medical emergency, Connor had pestered him until he agreed to have a pint with him.

Considering the fact that Connor and Shane had taken him to the doctor and helped him not embarrass himself even more in front of Karla, he couldn't refuse them. She'd looked at him with such pity, if he had pissed himself, he would never be able to look Karla in the eye ever again.

The doctor had been kinda nice too. Used to treating athletes, he also had a little experience dealing with amputees, so he'd given Jack a shot, and antibiotics with an order to finish the dose. He told him to wait until the swelling had gone down before he put on his prosthesis again.

On the car ride back to Jack's, Shane had been adamant that they sort his driving leg so that this didn't happen again. Jack wanted to protest, and yet, when Shane explained that Luke would need some time to be with Emil, and Noah had approved that anything else could wait. Jack was grateful that no one was getting on his case for being so stupid about the infection in his stump, and were actively trying to help him, and give him time to recover.

Fumbling with his keys, Jack balanced on his crutches, and then managed to get the door open. Moving inside, Jack closed the door, and made his way into the living room. He stopped dead when he came into the living area. Karla was curled up on his couch, her hands pillowed under her head, that dark hair of hers almost covering her face. Her legs were pulled up, and she had kicked off her shoes. Her beautiful face looked serene. She must have been absolutely wrecked with everything with Emil and now this...

Why was she still here though?

Jack tried to move quietly, grabbing the blanket on the back of the couch and clumsily draped it over her. Karla shifted slightly, and Jack froze, not wanting to disturb her. Seeing Karla in his space, sleeping on his couch, it unfurled something inside of him that he hadn't known that he was capable of.

Jack wanted this. He wanted Karla. He wanted someone to care enough about him that they stayed and waited for him to come home. He wanted Karla in his home, in his bed, in his fucking life and it terrified him a little,

He was used to being by himself...he wasn't used to letting people in.

Karla shifted in her sleep again, yawned, and then sat up. She rubbed her eyes and said something in Danish that Jack couldn't understand. He smiled as she woke, seemed to realize she hadn't spoken in English, and gave a sheepish smile.

"I'm sorry. I was waiting to see how you are and I fell asleep."

Jack set his crutches to the side and then sat down on the end of the sofa. "You didn't have to stay."

"I wanted to."

Silence descended between them, as Karla watched him, and Jack wasn't sure what to say next. Jack ran a hand through his hair, glanced at the door, then back at Karla. "You need me to call you a cab?"

"Are you trying to get rid of me?" Karla said with a husky laugh that shot a hell of a lot of blood to a part of his anatomy that made him glad for the loose hoodie over his joggers.

"No... I mean...shit...I'm sorry."

That made Karla chuckle again, then she glanced down at his stump. "What did the doctor say?"

Right...the real reason she was here...his stupidity.

"Um, ya," Jack started, rubbing a hand up and down his thigh. "Because the driving leg didn't fit right, it's just the skin and the friction that just made it worse. The doc gave me an injection to kick start the healing or whatever and he gave me antibiotics. Ordered me to take all me antibiotics this time round."

"You could have made yourself very ill, Jack."

Jack huffed out a breath. "Ya I know. Believe me. Shane and Connor already gave me a lecture on the way to the doctor's and back. Connor said he'd check in, and so did Shane. I guess I'm not used to people looking out for me."

Karla gave him a small smile. "And now you have me also."

From the way Karla said it, Jack couldn't help but feel like she meant it in a professional way and not in the way Jack was starting to think when he was with her.

"Ya, as my PR manager."

Karla frowned at the sharpness in his tone, which he hadn't meant to come out like that. "As your friend. We can be friends, Jack."

Hearing Karla say to him that they could be friends hurt worse than the pain in his stump. She had seen him on the floor and now, instead of looking at him with heat or lust, Karla would only pity him. Jack knew in the end that it was for the best because he wasn't the kind of guy that Karla deserved.

Jack told himself that he would stop being a dick to her.

And he would try and swallow the bitter pill of being her friend.

"Is Emil, okay?" Jack asked, ready to change the subject.

"It will be an adjustment," Karla told him, shifting so that she faced him, resting her head against the back of the couch. "But the doctors have assured him that he could return to football if he does what he is told. Luke is staying with him to make sure he takes it easy for a few days."

Jack knew she must have been through the wringer the last couple of days and then to come and see him sprawled out like a damn fool. He wouldn't be surprised if she high-tailed it back to Denmark to settle down with a Viking-looking dude who had all his limbs attached.

Jack frowned, his gaze narrowing at the thought of it.

"Jack?"

Jack shook himself from his thoughts as Karla said his name. "Ya?"

"Perhaps we should talk about what happened? The kiss?"

Swallowing hard, trying to ignore the flare of heat that flared in his neck and face, Jack scrubbed a hand down his face as he gave an embarrassed laugh. "Nah, it's all grand. It was the adrenaline, the thrill of going that fast and shit. I know it meant nothing so we should just forget that it ever happened and leave it at that."

Karla blinked, long lashes fanning her high cheekbones before she looked at him. "If that is what you want."

Jack wanted to shake his head and tell her no, that wasn't what he fucking wanted. All his life all he had wanted was to drive an F1 car, then a rally car. He had never wanted anything else as much, and then Karla had come crashing into his life, driving him fucking crazy and now, Jack wanted her.

Karla must have seen something in his eyes because she rose, and disappointment flooded through him for a moment, then he almost groaned when Karla climbed into his lap, leaned in and pressed her lips against his. Jack felt her tongue flick against the seam of his lips, and he opened for her, was rewarded with a hot, wet, kiss that had a moan lodged in his throat.

"What's...happening?" Jack asked through gritted teeth when they broke apart.

"I'm kissing you." Karla said like it should be obvious to Jack. She moved one hand from the front of his hoodie to the back of his neck, and into his hair. Jack felt like his skin was on fire, and not because he was fighting an infection.

Karla's fingers stilled as she lifted her head to look at him. "Should I stop?"

Stop? Was she fucking mad?

Jack knew there was no way he was calling a halt to this. He skimmed his hands from her curvy hips, along her spine, and when Karla shivered against his touch, Jack felt like he might explode if he didn't get her naked.

"No. Absofuckinglutely not." Jack told her, delighted when she laughed in a husky tone that went right to his dick. His hands came to rest just under her breasts. "But I just wanted to make sure you didn't want to wait, until, like, I can put my prosthetic back on?"

Chapter Twenty-Four

Karla

KARLA'S HEART clenched at the uncertainty in Jack's tone. It made her wonder who had made this cocky, self-assured man doubt himself. Like she would be revolted to see him naked or see him as less of a person, less of a man, with his limb missing.

"We can wait."

Karla rocked forward, making Jack groan. "Does that feel like I would like to wait?"

She watched as Jack swallowed hard, but there was no denying the lust in his eyes.

Karla leaned forward again, her lips on his jaw, the harshness of his stubble making her arch into him again, and Jack cupped her breast, his fingers teasing her nipple. She wanted the feel of his fingers against her skin without the barrier of clothes.

"Karla."

She lifted her eyes to look at Jack. His green eyes were

focused on her as he said. "Listen, I uh, some women like the idea of being with an athlete, and then there's me...knowing my leg is missing and then seeing it when I'm naked, it's... different."

Karla gave a quick peck on the lips, then shimmied off his lap. She could see the disappointment in his eyes. Tugging at the end of his shorts, Jack automatically lifted his hips and Karla gently pulled them down and tossed them aside. She could see Jack's erection straining against the black of his boxers, the head poking out of the waistband.

She had never been shy in the bedroom, and had liked being assertive. Her previous lovers had all liked her being assertive too, so Karla hoped that Jack didn't mind her taking the lead on this. Before dropping to her knees before Jack, she paused to strip off her tee, then her pants, leaving her in just her bra and knickers.

Jack groaned as he looked at her, which gave her a thrill, watching him lick his lips. Karla put her palms on his thighs, ran them up and down, then leaned in to press a kiss to the skin just above Jack's knee. The shudder that rippled through his body made Karla smile against his flesh.

Karla trailed her lips along the curve of his stump, careful to not touch anywhere that might be sore, continuing to massage her hand up and down his thighs. Then she moved her lips upward, toward his cock. Jack was breathing hard, his hands gripping the couch as she grinned at him.

"One of the first things I noted about you was how strong you were. Muscular arms, toned stomach, and I never once thought that you would look anything but delicious naked." She dipped a hand inside her knickers, brushed her fingers against the wetness and moaned.

"Fuck me." Jack ground out and Karla laughed.

"I intend to."

Jack's mouth hung open and Karla laughed.

"Do you have condoms?" She asked him, unhooking her bra and letting it fall to the ground.

"Top drawer in the bedside table. There's a pack in there."

Karla stripped off her knickers and kicked them off, heard Jack swear again as she walked into the bedroom and came back with the condoms. Jack was running his hand up and down his shaft, but he stopped when Karla came back out.

She set the pack of condoms on the arm of the couch and climbed onto his lap, her hand covering his as she made him stroke himself. Jack leaned forward, taking her breast in his mouth, Karla's free hand landing on his shoulder to steady herself as pleasure coursed through her.

Jack's teeth grazed her nipple and Karla threw her head back and squeezed his cock.

"Fuck, Karla, sweetheart, keep doing that and I'm not gonna last."

She teased him just a little by giving him one last stroke before she reached for the condom box. "Next time, I want to take you in my mouth, swallow you so deep that I can feel you at the back of my throat. Then I'll suck and lick, until you come."

Jack's cock twitched against her. "Fuck, how are you even real?"

Karla tore open the condom wrapper, then rolled it over Jack's shaft. Then he snaked a hand around to cup her neck, and pulled her in for a smouldering kiss that curled her toes.

Jack's calloused hands ran down her skin, the rough touch exactly what Karla wanted. She shifted her body so that Jack could feel how wet and ready she was for him, his muscles bunching under her touch as he tore his mouth from hers.

His hands slid down to grip her hips, to stop her from moving, when she would have lifted off and then taken Jack into her body. Pain flared in his eyes, and he slammed those pretty green eyes closed to try and hide it from her.

"Are you okay?" Karla whispered against his lips, holding onto his strong shoulders.

His hands tightened on her hips. "Just keep kissing me," Jack ground out, his next words coming out in a sexy growl. "I want you so much."

There is a rawness in Jack's tone that made Karla shudder. "You do?"

"So fucking much," Jack groaned against Karla's lips a moment before he kissed her again, hard, hot, possessive, his hands sliding down to cup her ass, bringing her closer to his hardness. "Since you showed up in the garage wearing those tight fucking jeans and that blouse that teased me with those fucking perfect tits of yours."

Karla laughed, shaking her head, then she took Jack's cock in her hand, held it as she lifted off his body and then with the blunt head at her entrance, lowered herself down. Inch by inch, Jack arching upward, her walls stretching to accommodate his thickness, Karla pushed past the pain to the pleasure until she needed to feel him inside her completely.

The next time Jack thrust into her, she lowered herself all the way and they both groaned at the sensation. Jack buried his face in between her breasts, his hands loosening on her hips to give her freedom to move.

Karla braced one hand behind her on his thigh, the other firmly grasping his shoulder as she slowly began to ride him. There was a slow burn between her legs, and Karla quickened her pace, lifting off and then slamming back down in a way that had them both breathing hard.

Her orgasm was building, and when Jack reached between them to pinch her clit, Karla's body rippled with pleasure, her orgasm hitting her like an arctic blast that had her gasping. Jack was still arching into her, prolonging the way her pussy clenched around his cock, and then his arm was around her waist.

That strength she had spoken about was evident in the way he twisted them so that her back was on the couch, Jack's weight holding her down. Jack pulled all the way out of her, then slammed into her so hard the couch moved. Jack kissed her as he began to thrust, hard and fast, then he buried his face in the crook of her neck, and Karla locked her legs around his waist as his pace became erratic, and frantic and she knew he was close to tethering over the edge.

Karla was also close to the edge again, the feel of Jack's hips hitting hers, the sound of his pants, and the feel of his breath on her skin, made her chase her release again until it hit her, even harder than her last one. Her inner muscles clenched and then Jack's body gave one last powerful thrust before he groaned her name and came.

After a couple of moments, Jack lifted his head, and kissed her slow and long, like they had all the time in the world. They stayed there, in each other's arms, then Karla shifted, and Jack pulled out of her, making her legs tremble just a little.

She laughed when he swore, and then took off the condom, reaching behind him to toss it in the bin. He looked at her, like he was expecting her to pick up her clothes and walk out the door. But Karla was not going anywhere.

"I'm going to the bathroom, and then I think I'll take a bath. That shower of yours looks big enough for two." Karla winked at Jack as he scrambled off the couch, reaching for his crutch, and the box of condoms.

Jack gave Karla this boyish sort of grin that flipped her stomach. "I feel like I've been conned here. I was expecting this coy, Danish princess but nah, man, you're a fucking vixen. A sexy fucking vixen."

That made her laugh as she went into the bathroom and closed the door behind her so she could relieve her bladder, then she opened the door, to find Jack leaning against the wall opposite the door.

He smiled at her, then used his crutch to come forward, then threw it aside to kiss her, moving so that they were inside the bathroom, still slick from sweat from the sex they had just had, and then Jack shut the door behind them, and they got sweaty and wet all over again.

CHAPTER TWENTY-FIVE

Jack

"JACK, do you want coffee or tea?"

Jack grinned as he pulled on a pair of shorts. "Tea, please."

He had Karla hadn't left his apartment in days. After their first night together, Karla had gone back to hers to get some stuff, and Jack had fully expected her to not come back. It wasn't because the sex had been bad, it had been fucking out of this world and Karla was unlike any woman he'd ever been with.

Jack couldn't help but think that like the other woman he's sort of dated, once the shiny wore off and the reality set in, they'd run so fast they'd outrun Usain Bolt. But Karla had come back, a duffel in her hand like she planned to stay a while, and a bag of shopping.

They had spent a lot of time in bed, on the floor, in the shower, and testing out the sturdiness of his furniture. Karla had cooked last night, and they'd eaten curled up on the couch watching some movie that Jack had no clue about because he'd been looking at her.

Using his crutches, Jack came out into the living room and kitchen area to see Karla dancing along to a tune on the radio, wearing one of his tee's and she looked sexy as fuck. The hem of it hit just below her thighs, and it made him want to lift her up and bury his face between her legs.

He had learned that was the quickest way to get her to swear in Danish at him.

As if she sensed where his mind had gone Karla rolled her eyes, then slid a plate of eggs and toast toward him. Jack perched up on one of the stools and ate his breakfast, absolutely ravenous. Karla came to sit beside him, and Jack reached out and rested a hand on her thigh, rubbing his thumb along her skin as he ate.

"I have to go to the office today. Shane has a few things for me to look over."

Jack knew that they would have to come out of their bubble at some stage, and back to reality, and he didn't know what exactly Karla wanted or where she wanted this to go. He lifted his hand off her leg, pushing his eggs around on his plate.

Karla reached out and brushed the hair from his face. "I plan on telling Shane about us. I do not know if it means I cannot work with you anymore or if Shane will be okay with it, but I do not wish to be dishonest."

Jack shifted around in his chair. "I mean, if this was just a hook-up, then you don't have to tell Shaney anything."

Karla's gaze narrowed as she arched a brow. "Was this just a hook-up for you?"

Fuck...he wasn't doing this right, was he?

Jack rubbed at the back of his neck. "I'm not good at words, Karla. I'm sorry."

She gave him a small smile. "Just be honest, Jack. That is all I can ask of you."

Taking a deep breath, Jack considered his words before he

said. "No. This wasn't just a hook-up. I want to give this, us, a shot. I'm not used to letting people in and I may act like a røvhul from time to time."

Karla gave him a sexy smile. "I promise to call you out if you are being an asshole."

Jack snorted, just her smile just unfurled some of the unease in his stomach. "I'm not going to give ya the poor me sob story, Karla. I've just had to rely on myself for so long. I didn't have the same kind of support that you had growing up. My Da was an abusive, drunk, SOB, and me Ma, she was a fucking pushover who let him be a shitty human being."

Karla reached over and put a hand on his knee, although she didn't say anything.

"I don't have siblings, and for the longest time, I was defined by racing. Then as an amputee. But this, you and me, I don't want to fuck it up but I don't know how to do this and not fuck things up."

She leaned in then to press a kiss to his jaw. "There is no pressure from me, Jack. Day by day. All that I ask is that you be honest with me if something does not feel right, or something is worrying you. I promise to do the same."

Jack cupped her cheek and kissed her, then his smile faltered. "Your brother's gonna fucking cut off my dick."

Karla chuckled, kissed him, and then got up off her stool with a wink. "I hope not. I am quite fond of your dick."

Jack burst out laughing as Karla went into the bathroom, and he heard the shower running. He was really fucking tempted to join her, convince her not to go to work, but he'd been selfish and kept her here for too long.

As much as he had been against Karla being his minder, it made him grin to think that no matter where he went, she'd be going too. He wouldn't have to miss her when he was off rallying, because she would be there, by his side.

If Shane thought he was gonna fire her, then Jack would just have to convince him otherwise.

Jack heard the shower turn off, then Karla came out in a towel, and headed for the bedroom. Jack grabbed his crutches, made his way into the bedroom, leaned in the doorframe as he watched her dress. Black lace boy shorts and a black bra were the first to go on, then Jack held back a groan as she shimmered her curves into those tight fucking jeans of hers.

She turned, glancing over her shoulder at him as she pulled them all the way up, then walked over to his chest of drawers and pulled out one of his NLQ tee's. Karla pulled it on over her head, the t-shirt too big for her, but then she did some elaborate knot on the end and then she swept her damn curls off her shoulder and put her hands on her hips.

"Do I look like a rally driver's girlfriend?"

Jack chuckled, rolling his eyes. "You know you look smokin', Karla. And don't be thinking about being any other rally driver's girlfriend."

"Well, I only know two rally drivers and one of them is with brother so I have no other options." Karla said with lots of sass.

Jack rolled his eyes, as

Karla strutted over to him, put her hands on the side of his neck. "Just yours, Jack O'Neill. I am yours."

Jack liked the sound of that. They kissed slowly, hands touching places that made the kiss get heated really quickly. It was Jack who broke the kiss, stepped back.

"You sure you gotta go to work?"

Karla tilted her head to the side. "Unfortunately. I can come back after I meet with Shane."

Jack grabbed a hoodie from the chair next to the bedroom door and pulled it on. "I'll drive ya over. I can come in and talk to Shane if ya want."

Karla grabbed her handbag, then held out her hand to Jack. "I'll be okay. Are you sure you should be driving? Is your leg okay?"

Jack shrugged, slipping his fingers into Karla's. "Swelling's gone way down. I need to try and put it back on at some stage. Come on. Let me drive ya."

Karla nodded, and she waited while Jack sat down on the couch and he rolled on the stump stock, bit back a wince as Karla handed him his prosthetic. Jack grinned thinking it was way different then the first time he and she had been holding his prosthetic. Karla held out her hand and he clasped it, helping him up.

When she was certain that he was okay to put weight on it, they went out to his car, then Karla placed her palm on his leg as he drove, and Jack felt ridiculously fucking happy. When he pulled up outside Rebel PR, he killed the engine.

"Gimmie a call when you're done, and I'll come get ya. Maybe we could eat out tonight so we might actually get through a meal without us getting naked."

Karla laughed, undid her seatbelt, and climbed onto Jack's lap. His hands went to her ass immediately, and he squeezed. Her hands went into his hair and then their mouths were fused together, this insatiable hunger for each other making Jack forget that they were in a public place and all he wanted to do was take her home and sink himself into her.

Jack broke the kiss with a groan, rested his forehead against Karla's. "You are a very bad influence, Karla Anderson."

"It can be our secret, Jack O'Neill. Just our secret."

Jack lifted his gaze to see Shane leaning against the door-frame, an amused expression on his face as he arched a brow at Jack.

"I think the secret's out, babe."

Karla glanced over her shoulder, then burst out laughing, burying her face against Jack's shoulder, and then he was laughing too, and it was the most Jack had laughed in fucking forever.

Chapter Twenty-Six

Karla

A WEEK after getting caught by Shane making out with Jack in his car, Karla hurried across the road, late for her lunch with Luke. Her brother's boyfriend was just after arriving back to Cork after spending time with Emil, who was staying on in the UK for another couple of days before coming back after he went to a doctor's appointment.

He was coping well with his new normal, Emil had told her, however Luke would tell her honestly how Emil was dealing with his health issues. Having talked it over with Jack, Karla had decided to wait until she and Emil were face-to-face before she told him that she and Jack were seeing each other.

Shane had been surprisingly accepting of their relationship. Once Karla had stopped laughing and gone inside, Karla had stood firm that while she hadn't meant for anything to happen with Jack, however now that it had, she promised it would not affect their working relationship.

It was Shane who had smiled and shrugged, telling Karla that she would get no judgement from him or even Andi, considering they were both dating their clients. He had just given her an already printed out piece of paper, to declare her and Jack's relationship in case anyone made a fuss.

She had asked him not to tell anyone else, other than Andi, until they were ready and Karla had spoken to her brother. Shane had nodded, but told Karla that he and Eve didn't keep secrets, so if she asked, he would tell her.

She just hoped that she would get the chance to sit down with Emil before the gossip got around. Jack had been very understanding of her wanting to keep things under wraps from any media, until they had told their families.

Jack had been a little reluctant to talk about his mother, and when he told Karla that he didn't want to taint one of the only good things in his life by visiting the absolutely rotten part of his past. Karla had hugged him then, telling him that he needed to make peace with his mother, and by realizing that as much as Jack was a victim of his dad's actions, his mother was also a victim too.

There had been a frown on Jack's face when he considered her statement, then he had gotten up off the couch and mumbled that he needed a minute, stalking off to his bedroom. Karla had simply turned on one of her Korean shows that Jack hated, but still watched with her and left him to sort things out in his head.

Half an hour into her episode, Jack had come out, gotten them both a can of soda from the fridge, and sat down beside her. His shoulder brushed against hers, and he waited until her episode was done before he spoke.

"I texted me Ma. I told her I'd call round next week."

"That's good."

"Maybe." That was all Jack had said but he had kissed her cheek, and pressed play on the next episode.

Jack had dropped her off before he went to work on his

car, and she rushed inside Rebel Books to meet Luke. He got up when he saw her coming and gave her a hug.

"I'm sorry I'm late."

Luke grinned and then sat down again. "It's grand. I was having a look around at some of the books. You want a coffee?"

"Please," Karla said as she took a seat and then Luke was smiling at a curvy blonde woman who was absolutely gorgeous as she was passing by the table.

"Hey Sorcha can we get two americanos and two of those gingerbread things if they haven't all been snapped up."

The blonde grinned at Luke. "Sure thing. Emil okay?"

"He's getting there. Sorcha this is Karla, Emil's sister."

Karla gave Sorcha a smile. "Nice to meet you."

Mischief danced in the woman's eyes. "Oh I've heard all about you from Eve. She's been meaning to ask ya to come out with us some night."

Of course the woman knew Eve. But it was hard to figure out how a bookseller knew an MMA fighter. Karla must have looked confused because Sorcha laughed, and tossed her blond hair off her shoulders.

"Oh I know that look. One thing you learn about living in Cork is that everyone is one step away from knowing someone else. Like for instance, I know Luke because my business partner is the sister of one of the lads in Heartache Melody, so our paths crossed and I know Eve, because she is cousins with one of the lads who works in Rebel Ink, across the road, who is dating Nessa, one of our managers."

Karla's head was starting to hurt.

"And I'm engaged to Ronan who is best friends with Shane who Eve is dating."

Karla burst out laughing, as Sorcha winked and headed off to get their coffees. "Is she telling the truth? It sounds like a massive soap opera."

"Ya, that just about sums it up," Luke replied with a grin, then gave her a sheepish kind of look.

"What?"

"I know, Karla."

Karla arched her brows. "Know what?"

Luke frowned, then sighed. "Remember when you video-called Emil the other night?" Karla nodded and then Luke continued. "You weren't at home when you called us."

Karla's eyes widened before she had the chance to school her expression. She considered lying, but had she not come here to tell Luke that she was seeing his teammate?

"No, when I called you I was not at home." She agreed with him.

Luke didn't say anything as Sorcha came back with their coffees and biscuits, then he added a sugar to his coffee before taking a sip, then he gave her a smile. "I recognised the couch. And the hoodie you were wearing."

Karla's mouth hung open, then she sighed. "Does Emil know?"

Luke shook his head. "Not that it's Jack, but he knew you were wearing a man's hoodie. He asked me if I knew of anyone that you had shown interest, and so as not to stress him out, I said I hadn't seen you with anyone in a romantic way and it's not a lie."

Karla reached across the table and gave his hand a squeeze. "I'm gonna tell him when he comes to Cork next week."

"Good," Luke replied with a grin. "I'm not surprised though. When we were in Manchester, you could feel the tension between you two, and then, Jack didn't leave your side when Emil had his cardiac event."

Luke lifted his coffee to his mouth, swallowed, then looked at Karla. "Is he good to you? Because that's what Emil will want to know. It's what I wanted to know when Luna started dating Cathal, but you just had to see the two of them together to see that he worships the ground she walks on, and she adores him. I know he can be a bit standoffish and that, but I used to be a little like that with people I didn't know. And you two didn't hit it off to begin with."

"He hasn't been anything but good to me. I would stand for nothing less." Karla told Luke as he sat back in his seat. "And yes, he is a little standoffish, and we clashed when we first met, however beneath all that prickly exterior, is a man who has lived a hard life. He doesn't let people in, but when he does, he is funny, and smart, and makes me laugh."

Karla felt her lips curve into a smile and Luke was looking at her with a knowing smile. "I see it now- You're in love with him."

She hadn't thought about it up until then, had known she had strong feelings for Jack, but up until Luke had pointed it out, she had not realized just how fast she had fallen. It was a little terrifying to come to that realization, considering they were just getting to know one another. But there was no denying the truth of it all.

"I guess I am. Or falling might be a better word to use. I hate to ask, but can you forget we've discussed this? I think Jack deserves to know how I feel before anyone else."

Luke grinned, his eyes dancing. "At least you get to declare your love without the added pressure of coming out of the closet. Does he feel the same way do you think?"

Karla hoped that Jack did feel the same about her however he guarded his feelings ... in a way, despite the easy smile and sense of humour, Jack reminded her of Oskar, who had always seemed so closed off to his emotions. But Oskar had changed since meeting his Quinn...and Jack was trying with her...but would Jack drive as fast as he could away when he realized things were getting serious between them? Karla hoped that the demons of Jack's past, did not become the one thing to put a grinding halt to their future.

Chapter Twenty-Seven

Jack

JACK PULLED into the drive of his family home and killed the engine. Unbuckling his belt, Jack leaned his head against the headrest. He'd been dreading this all week, and if it hadn't been for Karla, then he probably would have texted his Ma to tell her something came up and avoid revisiting all the pain that came with stepping over the threshold of that house.

For years Jack didn't understand why his Ma hadn't sold the house and gotten something smaller for herself. He was partially to blame for that, needing adjustments made to the house to accommodate Jack's needs. But when Jack moved out, she could have sold the gaff, and moved on with her life.

Jack saw the curtain twitch, and knew his Ma was checking to see if Jack was actually gonna come into the house. His phone pinged, and he picked it up, and then smiled.

Go inside. Everything will be grand xx

Karla was fucking amazing. And far too good for him, but Jack wasn't a fool to let her go. Right now, Karla was meeting up with Emil and Luke, and telling her brother about their relationship, and Jack was going to bite the bullet and go and see his Ma.

Getting out of the car, Jack considered what Karla had said to him last week. He'd never even considered the things his Ma had gone through because of his Da. He'd only thought that she was weak, unable to leave her alcoholic husband because of it. He had blamed his Ma, and taken his anger out on her.

Jack knew it was because his Da wasn't here for Jack to take his anger out on. As much as he cursed his Da on the daily, his Ma had tried to overcompensate for what she had said when he first woke from his coma, and realized his leg was gone. And her smothering had just fanned the flames of his rage.

Walking up to the front door, Jack knocked, and then used his key to open the door. His palms were sweaty, and for some reason, Jack had a bundle of nerves coiled in his stomach. Jack moved through the hall, glancing at pictures of him as a kid, with his trophies and medals. Jack stopped at the picture of Jack when he won his first karting championship, and he couldn't remember the feeling of joy like that kid had in his eyes.

"Jack. I've made tea and got in some of those biscuits you like." Jack turned to see his ma standing in the doorway. "I wasn't sure if you were on one of your training diets, but I have low-fat stuff as well, if you'd prefer."

Jack gave his Ma a grin. "Nah, biscuits be grand. I'll do some extra push-ups to work it off. You didn't need to get anything in especially."

"It was nothing. Come in, take a seat."

Jack followed his Ma into the living room, where his Ma had laid out some tea and biscuits. She sat down and wrapped her cardigan around herself. As Jack took his seat, he was suddenly very aware of how small his Ma was. It wasn't something that Jack had ever really focused on before.

Jack came bounding in from school, and stopped dead when he saw his Ma picking up the remains of what used to be her teapot. It was the one his nan had before she died and meant a lot to his Ma. She was on her hands and knees, sweeping up the shattered fragments.

"Ma?"

His Ma lifted her head. Jack saw that her eyes were red, her skin blotchy like it got when she'd been crying. Her eyes went wide, and she tried to hide her lip but Jack had already seen the cut that he knew had come from his Da's open palm.

"I'm okay, I slipped, and it fell out of my hand."

Jack didn't believe her, and he was about to call her out on it when he heard the back door fly open and his Da came in, tossing his cigarette in the sink. "Go and go your homework, lad. Your Ma will call ya for dinner."

He stood there and looked at his Ma. His Da started forward and Jack braced, when his Ma was suddenly between them, and she gave Jack a smile that didn't quite meet her eyes. "Go on, Jack. I'm making pork chops. They won't be long."

"Jack?" Jack blinked and lifted his eyes to his Ma. They had the same colour eyes, he and his Ma, and she was looking at him with a worried expression.

"I'm sorry, Ma."

"What for, Jack?"

Jack ran a hand through his hair. "For being an asshole. For blaming you for what happened to me, for blaming you for staying with Da, for pushing you away while I tried to come to terms with losing my F1 dream."

"You don't need to apologise, Jack. You were a child." His Ma told him. However, Jack shook his head.

"I do, Ma, I really fucking do. I was here too, and I saw the bruises, the cut lips. I was blinded by how much I hated what

147

had happened to me that I forgot how often you stepped in so he didn't lamp me one. Someone very smart told me that as much of a victim I was of Da, so were you."

His Ma's eyes widened, a sheen of tears in her eyes. "It's okay, Jack. I'm your mother. It was my job to protect you and I failed. I failed when I didn't leave when he first lashed out. I failed when I didn't take you and run far away. I let you down when I got in that car and it almost killed you."

A tear rolled down her cheek and Jack had to swallow his own tears.

"I was a terrible mother when I let my grief over losing one child, stop me from sitting by the bedside of my other child. And I failed you when my guilt made me blame you, when I couldn't blame the man who almost took both my children from me."

His Ma sobbed, and covered her face with her hands. Jack hated to see her cry. Jack got up off the chair, and went over to her, sitting down on the arm of the chair, and wrapped his arms around her. It was the first time he'd hugged his Ma since before the accident.

Jack hadn't realized how much he had missed it...missed her.

"It's okay, Ma. It's okay."

She patted his back and lifted her head, giving him a small smile. "You haven't hugged me in years. You used to be my huggy baby. Until you were old enough to understand what your Da was. And then you closed yourself off from me and I told myself it was keeping you safe. It was what I clung to, when you started to look at me like you hated me."

Jack swiped at his eyes. "I'm sorry, Ma. I really am. I want to try and rebuild, if you want."

"I would like that very much, Jack."

Jack grinned, then went over to his seat and grabbed a biscuit, then tossed it into his mouth while his Ma poured the tea. They sat there in silence for a few minutes, the distance between them still lingering because it had been years since they had a civil conversation.

"I read online that you were about to become a rally driver."

Jack nodded, his grin deepening. "Ya, I thought that I'd never get to do it, Yano? To race for a living, but Noah's been good to me. Took a chance on me. And I love it."

"And it's safe?" His Ma asked.

"I won't lie and say it's perfectly safe, but everything is done to make sure me and Luke are safe. You could come to the race track one day maybe, have a look yourself."

"If you want me to, then I will."

They lapsed into silence again, but Jack knew that it would take time for this to get easier, that the tension and the hurt couldn't be erased with one cuppa and a biscuit.

"Jack, why now? after all this time, why can you forgive me now?"

Jack set his mug down on the table, and gave his Ma a smile. "Like I said, a very smart person made me see things a little differently. She's made me see a lot of things differently."

His Ma put her hand on her chest, and gave him a smile that reminded of him of the Ma he remembered when he was too small to know what was going on. She released a breath, then said. "What's her name? I think I'd like to meet her someday."

A couple of weeks ago, Jack would never have even considered that one day, he'd be sat across from his Ma, talking about the woman in his life, and laying the foundations of a new relationship that might come out of it.

"Her name's, Karla," Jack told his Ma, unable to hold back his grin. "And I think I fucking love her."

Chapter Twenty-Eight

Jack

KARLA HAD TOLD Jack that that Emil had seemed okay with the fact that the two of them were seeing each other. He knew that his track record, his piss poor attitude wouldn't have done him any favours, but while he wanted Emil to take them seriously, it was Karla's opinion that mattered.

When he'd come home after seeing his Ma, Karla had listened to him, then gave him a quick kiss and told him that she was proud of him. Jack had asked her to come with him the next time he went over or try and arrange a dinner or something.

Shane had called Karla that same night and invited them to come over and watch the season opener for the F1 season. Charlie wanted everyone to watch with her since she couldn't be there in person. Karla had wanted to go, and Jack wanted to be with Karla, so they had agreed to go.

Jack had been quiet after they'd agreed to go, and Karla had run her fingers through his hair and asked him what was wrong. He hadn't really been sure what was wrong, but Karla, his amazing, confident, caring girlfriend, let him work it out in his head before he gave her a sheepish look.

"I'm sorry," Jack had said, to which Karla scrapped her nails over his scalp in the way he liked. "I'm being stupid."

"Nothing new there then." Karla had replied in a teasing tone, making him laugh and steal a kiss.

"This is going well...us. And I'm afraid the moment it's out in the open and everyone is in our business, that I'm gonna do something to fuck it up. And I really don't want to fuck this up, Karla."

She'd climbed into his lap and put her hands on his neck. "There are only two people who can, fuck this up, as you say. And as long as we talk things out, I think we will be grand."

Jack had tried to argue with her, or tell her to be serious, but she had taken off her top, and his brain had gotten all scrambled, and he'd forgotten all about his fears for a couple of hours, and just lost himself in her.

When Karla had left his place this morning to go to work, they had arranged to go for lunch after he got his workout done at the gym. It was the little things, the things that Jack hadn't had before that he liked doing the most. Besides all the sex that was, and the sex was definitely fanfuckingtastic.

He'd never had the movie nights, the making a meal together, the checking in during the day, or having someone sleep beside him at night. Last night, after Karla had fallen asleep, he'd lain awake and just held her, wondering how he had gotten so damn lucky.

Jack zipped up his hoodie, heard a knock on his front door, and grinned. There was no one else he was expecting, so he really hoped that Karla had finished up her meeting with Shane early so that they could finish off where they started this morning, with a kiss that melted his bones and the promise of a naked workout.

Tossing his keys on the counter, Jack walked toward the

door. "Couldn't even cope for a few hours without seeing me naked? You shoulda stayed so we could have finished what we start-"

Jack opened the door and immediately wished that the ground could swallow him up.

Emil stood on the other side of the door, a scowl on his face. "I would refrain from finishing that sentence if I were you."

Jack didn't know what to say. Karla's brother was not who he had been expecting to be on the other side of his front door, and now, like fuck if Jack knew what to say to him. He just stood there like a twat, completely unable to formulate a sentence.

"Luke brought me here. He's outside in the car since I'm not allowed to drive at the moment. I thought you and I could have a word."

Fuck.

Jack didn't know what to do in this situation. It was like he forgot how to be a civilized human. Emil and Karla were close. And his opinion mattered to Karla. Jack knew that if Emil didn't like Jack, that it would cause a rift between the siblings, and Jack would hate himself if he was the cause of it.

"Are you going to invite me in, or do you intend to let a man who has just had surgery stand out here all day?"

Jack stepped back and held the door open as Emil walked into his apartment. Jack closed the front door and tried to hold his nerve as he walked into the living area, and asked Emil if he wanted to sit. The footballer perched on the arm of one of the chairs and rested his hands in his lap.

His eyes though, they scanned the small apartment. Jack watched as he took in the few items belonging to Karla that were scattered around the place, from her Denmark hoodie to her hair curler thing, and the fluffy socks she liked to wear.

Emil shifted his gaze back to Jack. "What makes you think that you are good enough for my sister?"

This was an interrogation. A vetting. And Jack knew that Emil would make up his mind about him after talking to him about Karla. He could see where Karla had gotten her tough streak...

"I'm not." Jack told Emil, running his hand through his hair. "She is far too fucking good for me, and I know it. But for some reason, Karla likes me and to be honest, I'm not sure why."

Emil gave a slight inline of his head. "You are right, she is far too good for you."

"At least we can agree on that, I suppose."

Folding his arms across his chest, Emil held Jack's gaze. "I am protective over my sisters. When my father had his accident, and our mother fell apart, I looked after them. Karla is a strong, independent woman who can make her own mind up about who she wants to be involved with."

Jack thought it best to keep his mouth shut, and not say anything.

"Luke told me how you behaved when ye first met-"

"I was a prick." Jack interjected, feeling like he had to say something. "I had all these insecurities and hang ups. When I first lost me leg, they tried to saddle me with a carer. I was pissed off because I didn't want someone babysitting me. When Rebel PR hired Karla, it triggered me and I took it out on her."

"Well, at least you are man enough to admit it." Emil drawled, but Jack wasn't finished.

"My Da, was an alcoholic. I was an only child. I didn't have friends because I didn't want to have to lie about why no one could come to my house. And being an F1 driver was a way for me to get out. I react without thinking. If I'm being honest, I think I knew I had a thing for Karla and it terrified me. I tried to push her away but she didn't let me. I'm really fucking grateful she didn't though."

Emil's features softened. "Luke told me how you looked after Karla after my cardiac event. That tells me what I need to know, Jack. I will let Karla make her own mind up."

Karla's brother stood, and Jack felt compelled to do the same. "I also remember how you stood up for Luke when that reporter wanted to dig up dirt. You barely knew us and you stood up for us. And I know what it is like to love someone who is not used to letting people close. If Karla is trying with you, then she has to believe that you are worth it."

Jaysus, Jack fucking hoped so...he really did.

"Thanks, Emil, I know Karla will be glad that you approve."

Email chuckled, giving him an amused smile. "Not yet, but I might do one day. But Jack, I may have a piece of machinery in my chest now, but if you hurt her, if you cause her pain, then you will have to deal with me."

"If I hurt her, I'll let ya."

Emil strode toward the door, paused and said. "You might just do, Jack. You might just do."

Relief flooded through Jack and his shoulders sagged a little. "Oh thank Christ, I honestly thought that you were here to kill me for daring to touch her and bury me in some hole in the woods."

Emil gave him a smirk. "Not yet. And besides, with my heart condition, it would not be me that comes for you. I would simply call Oskar and he would do it. He is the one that was in the military after all. He loves Karla like a little sister."

Jack felt the colour drain from his face, and that made Emil laugh as he clasped Jack on the shoulder, gave it a squeeze. "Now, we understand each other."

CHAPTER TWENTY-NINE

Karla

KARLA FELT relaxed as she finished getting ready to head to Charlie's to watch the Grand Prix race. Last night, Luke and Emil, and her and Jack had gone for dinner, and despite Emil playing the overprotective brother for the first couple minutes until Karla kicked him under the table, it had gone well.

She had found it cute that Jack had been so nervous about the dinner. And he was a little on edge about today. Karla knew that it was because the last time they had been in Charlie's house together, they had called such a scene, and he was a little embarrassed.

Jack came out of the bedroom with a scowl on his face. "Is this the kind of thing we need to dress up for? I don't have anything fancy so it's jeans and a clean hoodie or shorts."

Karla laughed, slipped her feet into her trainers. Jack stopped as he came into the room, and she could feel the heat of his gaze on her. "You're wearing my fave bloody jeans. Are you trying to torture me?"

"Of course not," Karla replied, reaching for her own hoodie. "I just really like how good my ass looks in them."

Jack came over, and zipped up her hoodie, then reached around to slip his hands into the back pockets of her jeans. "I really like how good your ass looks in them too."

Smacking his chest, Karla arched up to kiss his jaw. "We will be late if we don't leave now."

Jack gave her a grin that told Karla he was thinking of getting her out of her jeans. "We could stay here, yano. No one will miss us."

Karla arched her brow, then said in a teasing tone. "Are you ashamed to be seen out with me?"

Jack snorted, rolling his eyes. "Fuck no. I can't wait until everyone knows you're my girl. Now that Emil knows and Shane, it's gonna get out. Best we do it our own way."

I can't wait until everyone knows you're my girl.

That statement alone made Karla's heart skip a beat. She knew Jack was worried about screwing things up between them, but if he kept saying things like that to her, she might just blurt out exactly how much she had fallen for him. It felt insane just how easily they had danced into this routine, considering where they first started.

Jack grabbed his keys, and they headed out. The drive to Charlie's house Jack was quiet, as Karla just put her hand on his thigh and left him to his thoughts. She had learned being with Jack that sometimes, they didn't need to say anything, and sometimes Jack just needed the quiet. She understood that about him just like he understood her need to decompress after a day of work.

The other night after back-to-back meetings, Karla had arrived home to her own house to a warm bathtub, a bottle of rosé she liked, and takeout waiting for her. Jack must have come over before he went for a session at the gym, and it had melted her heart.

Jack pulled into Charlie's drive and turned off the engine. "You ready for this?"

Karla nodded, getting out of the car and held out her hand to Jack. He slipped his fingers not hers, and it felt right, it felt good. Jack glanced at her then, his vivid green eyes twinkling as he lifted their hands, grazed her knuckles with his lips.

Jack opened the door and Karla stepped inside, waiting for Jack to close the door. Karla all but pulled him toward the kitchen. She let out a yelp when Jack yanked her back and kissed her. It was the kind of kiss she had gotten addicted to with Jack; hot, hard, and filled with a promise of decadent passion.

"I fucking knew it! I fucking called it! Pay up bitches. Eve needs a new pair of Jordans!"

Karla and Jack broke apart and turned to see Eve grinning at them, and the rest of their friends congregated in the doorway of the kitchen. The MMA fighter was giving gimmie hand gestures and every single person was handing her money.

Jack started laughing, shaking his head. "You lot are fucking awful, ya know that?"

Eve bounced out toward them and slung her arms around them. "Ya we are but damn, O'Neill, even a blind man could see the sexual fucking tension between you too. All that back and forth was fire...and I should know. How the hell do you think me and Shane hooked up?"

Ever grabbed Karla's hand and pulled her into the kitchen. She glanced over her shoulder, saw Jack's eyes on her, a cheeky smile curving his lips before Eve monopolized her attention, asking for all the details about her relationship with Jack.

Karla found herself laughing, when Eve asked her something rather raunchy and Emil, who had been sitting on the chair opposite them, frowned and got to his feet stating that he would rather not hear about his baby sister's sex life, lest he have another cardiac event.

To most, it might seem a bit macabre to joke about what had happened to him, but Karla knew her brother, and this was his way of coping, and trying to prove that he was okay with everything that had happened to him. Karla would keep an eye on him, as would Luke, but Emil would come to terms with things in his own way.

Charlie came to sit down beside her, resting her hand on her belly, and everyone soon grabbed a spot to watch the race. Karla glanced over her shoulder to see Jack laughing with Luke and Shane, and it made her smile.

"It'll be good for him," Charlie said as she saw where Karla was looking. "We were worried about him, me and Andi. We tried to get him involved in things like this. Luke tried. But he always looked like we'd invited him to have a tooth pulled."

Karla would not betray Jack's trust, but Charlie did sound genuinely worried. "I admit, he is not used to letting people see certain aspects of him. His life hasn't always been easy."

Charlie smiled, and ran a hand over her belly. "Noah was like that when my dad took him in. It took me ages to get him to warm up to me. Hell, I'm still waiting for him and Andi to warm to each other."

The woman in question came and sat down on the arm of the sofa, and nudged Charlie on the shoulder. "Me and Noah have an understanding now. And my fiancé kinda likes him as well so we have to be nice to one another. Our relationship means we pretend we don't like one another, but secretly Noah's not that bad...but if any of you tell him I said that I will deny it."

Everyone laughed at what Andi said, as the coverage started for the race, and Charlie turned up the volume. The camera's scanned the pit lane, and went directly to Noah, who was climbing into his car. Charlie grinned and Karla could see how in love she was with Noah.

Karla glanced up to see Jack come over with a drink for

her, and then he sat down beside her. She leaned against his shoulder as everyone gathered round with Emil sitting on a chair, Luke sitting on the ground in front of him. Eve was sat in Shane's lap on the other chair, and Karla was thrilled that this time round, it was already a far better outcome than the previous time.

Jack's lips brushed the top of her head and she shifted to look up at him. He smiled, and Karla knew right there and then, that she was in love with Jack. Karla had come to Ireland in search of a new life, to find herself and follow her own path. She had a job she loved. She had been welcomed by all these people with open arms and hearts.

But most of all, Karla had found Jack. She had never imagined that she could find someone who fit her so completely, and made her feel sexy, smart, and cared for. If she had been uncertain before of whether she had made the right decision to leave Denmark, being here tonight made her believe without a doubt that she had done the right thing.

"I'm glad we came." Jack said softly. "This is actually fun."

"More fun than getting me out of these jeans?" Karla said in a teasing tone.

Jack opened his mouth with a mischievous glint in his eyes, however, before he could utter a word, Emil cut across him.

"If you answer that, Jack, I will not be responsible for my actions."

Everyone in the room started to laugh, as Jack flushed and Karla hauled him down for a kiss, that had Emil swearing in Danish and Karla's heart felt so full, she knew now that Ireland was home for her. Because Karla was surrounded by love...

And a rally driver who had her heart.

Chapter Thirty

Jack

Three Weeks Later

Jack was surprised that he hadn't done something to fuck things up with Karla. Everything was going so bloody well that Jack was waiting for her to realize that she could do so much better than him. But for some reason, Karla seemed happy to be with him.

Karla was a social butterfly. She loved being around people, so Jack had made a conscious effort to step outside of his comfort zone and be more social. They had gone out with Shane and Eve, and Jack had even gone for a drink with Shane, Connor, and Ronan Cusack one night. Karla had even borrowed Luke's car to drop him off and collect him.

Jack had been surprised at how much he'd enjoyed hanging out with the lads.

Before Emil went back to the UK to work on his recovery, they had gone for Sunday dinner to Luke's parents' house. It had been super surreal to see how families *should* be, and he'd be lying if he said that he wasn't overwhelmed by it all.

Karla had seen the look on his face and reached for his hand under the table, especially when his leg started bouncing. He felt out of his depth and uncomfortable and he wanted to just go home, but Luke's mam had asked him to help her in the kitchen, and she'd made him wash the dishes.

Jack had done so, wondering why he had reacted so weirdly to seeing just how easily everyone interacted. But he supposed that it was down to never remembering having Sunday roasts, or dinners, when he and his Ma hadn't been on guard, waiting for his Da to get drunk.

When he had finished up, Luke's mam had wrapped her arms around him, and given him a hug. It had been years since Jack had hugged anyone and now everyone was fucking hugging him. Luke's mam hadn't said anything after she released him, just patted his cheek, telling Jack that there would always be a seat for him at the dinner table.

After they had gotten home, Jack had sat on the couch and just stared at the blank screen of the TV. Karla had made them both a cup of tea, then sat down beside him, putting a hand on his back and rubbing small circles on his back.

"Is that what it's like? Being a normal family?" Jack had asked Karla quietly.

Karla laughed, the sound tugging on his heart. "It was different in Denmark. I think Luke's family are special in how close they all are. However, the dinners, the hanging out, the movie nights, our friends do their own version of it. I believe they even spend Christmas time together or so Emil said."

He had shifted on the couch to look at her. "I'm sorry I was weird."

Karla had cupped his neck, and brushed her lips against his jaw. "You were not weird. The first time I went for dinner, I was surprised at how at ease they all were with one another. We are different in Denmark. But I like the Irish version of family. It would seem that there will always been friends or family eager to spend time with us."

He had seen it in her eyes that Karla was delighted to be surrounded with so many people, and while Jack would be happy to just spend his time with Karla or his car, he would continue to step outside his comfort zone just to see that beautiful smile on her face.

Yesterday, Jack had taken Karla to meet his Ma. When Jack had asked his Ma if he could bring Karla round to meet her, his Ma had insisted they come for afternoon tea. The moment Karla stepped inside his childhood home, she had gone to the photos and grinned as she scanned through them, claiming that he had been a gorgeous baby.

Jack had rolled his eyes, even as his Ma had come out of the kitchen, introduced herself to Karla, then told his girlfriend that she had albums full of pictures of Jack. Karla had seemed delighted, letting his Ma lead her into the living room, where she proceeded to pull out a fuckton of albums.

But he had been utterly shocked to see his Ma take out a scrapbook filled with articles about Jack, even after he had moved out. She had the press release in a local paper about him joining NLQ racing. Hell, she even had that embarrassing photo shoot that he had done because Shane had made him. They had ended up staying longer than Jack thought they would, and when Karla asked if they could order in some food, because she was enjoying hearing stories of Jack as a child, he had agreed.

Last night Jack had woken screaming, the phantom pains jerking him awake and his screams had woken Karla. When Karla had started to stay over or when he went to hers, Jack had explained to her about the phantom pain, and felt like an idiot as he explained about the mirror therapy intervention method, Karla had listened carefully to what he was explaining.

When Jack had finished, Karla had a very serious face when she asked him if he needed a specific mirror, or type of mirror, so that she could make sure that she had what he needed at her place. Karla had asked him to show her how the method worked, in case he couldn't get to his mirror.

After waking up screaming, Karla had seen that Jack was disorientated, and she had just slipped from the bed, grabbed the mirror from the bedside table, and held it in place while Jack just focused on the mirror. Karla then placed a hand on his knee, just above the stump, and it anchored him, and helped Jack to focus on her and not on the pain his brain was telling him that he was in.

Then Karla had climbed back into bed and held him until he had fallen asleep.

She hadn't mentioned what had happened as they had breakfast, or when they kissed goodbye before Karla went into Rebel PR, and Jack went up to Rebel Racers to work on his car. He had shown Karla a side that no one else saw. He'd let her see him at his most vulnerable, and she had not recoiled in horror. Jack had known then that Karla would never pity him for the fact that he was missing a limb, or for the stupid weird side effects that were a part of his trauma.

So it was no wonder that Jack arrived to work on his car with the biggest fucking grin.

His new and correctly fitted driving prosthetic had been installed in his rally car, so Jack tinkered with the car for a while, then unhooked his prosthetic, setting it aside before he hopped over to his car. Jack knew the moment he placed his stump into the cup that this wouldn't be the same as last time.

It felt good....he felt good.

Jack lost himself in the car, just pulled out of the garage and tore around the track like he was trying to get the fastest lap around the Nuremberg ring. He tested the car to see if her could drift, and the new driving leg worked like a treat. The car was feeling fanfuckingtastic and he was looking forward to getting it out on a proper stage.

When it started to get dark, Jack called it a day and made his way into the garage. Reversing in, Jack grinned when he saw his sexy brunette waiting for him. Jack parked the car, and opened the door, unhooking his stump after taking off his seatbelt. He turned in his seat to see Karla standing there, holding out his prosthetic to him.

Jack snorted as he remembered the day that they had met, and how their lives had changed. Instead of being horrified at him, Karla was giving him a warm smile that made him want to kiss her. Fuck that, Jack always wanted to kiss her.

Karla gave him a quizzical expression as he took the prosthetic from Karla, put it on, and then stood up to go to her, and he kissed her, just like he wanted to do. When they broke apart, Karla arched her brows, and it was then that Jack knew that this was exactly what he wanted from his life.

"I love you," Jack told Karla as her eyes widened. "I thought that you would drive me crazy, but I'm so glad that I didn't scare you off."

Karla cupped Jack's face, and Jack wrapped his arms around her. "I'm not easily frightened, Jack O'Neill. Even if you were a røvhul when we first met. And just so you know, I love you too."

As soppy as it sounded, Jack's heart felt like it was full...

Backing Karla up against the counter, Jack kissed her, showing her with his mouth, and his hands, just how much he wanted her, how much he needed her, trying to prove that he was worthy of her. Jack would work hard to prove to Karla every single day that he was the man she deserved. And Jack would try very hard not to be an asshole ....

Even if it sounded fucking sexy as hell coming from the woman he loved.

THE END

The Rebel County Universe Stories continue in
Up in Flames (Rebel Rescue Book 1)

Take The Lead is the third book in the Rebel Books Trilogy. Rebel Books is part of the Rebel County Universe which will span at least four different businesses, with intersecting timelines, and characters popping up when you least expect them.

The Rebel Racers Trilogy
Available Now:
Adrenaline Junkie (Rebel Racers Book 1)
All or Nothing (Rebel Racers Book 2)
Crash and Burn (Rebel Racers Book 3)

The Rebel Rock Trilogy
Available Now:
Centre Stage (Rebel Rock Book 1)
Strings Attached (Rebel Rock Book 2)
Make or Break (Rebel Rock Book 3)

The Rebel Ink Trilogy
Available Now:
Breaking the Habit (Rebel Ink Book 1)
Uncomfortably Numb (Rebel Ink Book 2)
Secrets In Ink (Rebel Ink Book 3)

The Rebel Books Trilogy
Available Now:
Best Laid Plans (Rebel Books Book 1)
More Than Words (Rebel Books Book 2)
Take The Lead (Rebel Books Book 3)

The Rebel PR Trilogy
Available Now:
Sucker For Pain (Rebel PR Book 1)
Drive Me Crazy (Rebel PR Book 2)

The Rebel Rescue Trilogy
Available Now:
Up in Flames (Rebel Rescue Book 1)

Playlists

JACK

Fine Young Cannibals - She Drives Me Crazy
Jaymes Young - What Is Love
Ellem - That Thing You Do (Lhotse Remix)
Måneskin - OFF MY FACE
Måneskin - THE DRIVER
Ed Sheeran - Magical
Lovejoy - Normal People Things
The Seige - I Am Defiant
Jack Kays - Caffeine
Sum 41 - Landmines
The Maine - thoughts i have while lying in bed
Dead Poet Society - Running In Circles
Nico Santos - Where You Are
Dead Poet Society - My Condition
Aslan - Crazy World
Wilkinson - This Moment
Teddy Swims - Lose Control
Stereophonics - Dakota
The Band CAMINO - I Think I Like You

YUNGBLUD - When We Die (Can We Still Get High?) (feat. Lil Yachty)

Cassyette - Why Am I Like This?

Juelz Santana - There It Go (The Whistle Song)

Karla

Britney Spears - (You Drive Me) Crazy

Julia Michaels - Heaven

Astræa - You're Not Alone - Acoustic

Ruth B. - Situation

Anica - tucked away

Raye Zaragoza - Still Here

The Last Dinner Party - Nothing Matters

The Beaches - Blame Brett

goddard. - Wasted Youth

Jonas Blue - Fast Car

Christopher - Bad

Christopher - When I Get Old

Rihanna - Shut Up And Drive

Clean Bandit - Drive (feat. Wes Nelson)

Silvana Imam - Tänd Alla Ljus

Florence + The Machine - Shake It Out

Taylor Swift - Is It Over Now? (Taylor's Version) (From The Vault)

Izzy Bizu - Dumb

Conan Gray - Killing Me

Calum Scott - Lighthouse

Justin Timberlake – Selfish

Moncrieff - False Alarm

ACKNOWLEDGMENTS

None of this would be possible without an amazing team supporting me! Many thanks to:

Publishing House: CTP Publishing
Cover design: Gem Promotions
Interior Formating: Gem Promotions

———

And as always:
Thank you to all the readers!
Whether this is your first book by me or you've been with me for years! I only get to do this because of you, and I am eternally grateful to each and every one of you who took a chance on this Irish author.

About the Author

Susan Harris is a writer from Cork, Ireland and when she's not torturing her readers with heart-wrenching plot twists or killer cliffhangers, she's probably getting some new book related ink, binging her latest TV or music obsession, or with her nose in a book.

Susan LOVES connecting with her fans!
www.susanharrisauthor.com

Also by Susan Harris

The Wings Of Deceit Series

Angel's Gambit, book 1

Angel's Rebel, book 2

Angel's Traitor, book 3

Angel's Shadow, book 4

The Ever Chace Chronicles

Skin & Bones, book 1

Collateral Damage, book 2

Smoke & Mirrors, book 3

Night of the Hunter, book 4

Never Back Down, book 5

Shortcut to the Grave, book 6

Arsonist's Lullaby, book 7

Of Gods & Monsters, book 8

———

Shattered Memories

———

Defy The Stars

A Tale of Two Houses, book 1

Until Death Do Us Part, book 2

In Defiance of the Stars, book 3

Courting Darkness, a novella

The Sanguine Crown

Chaos Theory, book 1

Butterfly Effect, book 2

Wicked Game, book 3

Burn Notice, book 4

Fight Song, book 5

The Sicarius Security Series

Kiss Of Death, book 1

Leap Of Faith, book 2

Visions Of Destiny, book 3

War Of Hearts, book 4

Flames Of Conflict, book 5

Anthology

A Lot Like Christmas

The Murdering Hour Novels

Own The Night, book 1

Dwell In Darkness, book 2